Quarantine with the Billionaire

DIAMONDS NICOLE WATSON

Dedications

First and foremost, I'd like to thank God for the gift of my imagination. I'd like to dedicate this book to my biggest supporters, Michael, my "twin" Tiffany, my amazing web designer Zam, my photographer Ryan, and Shirley-Ann for the unconditional, unwavering support of my work. To all my friends, thank you for continuing to inspire, uplift, and motivate me as I fight for my dreams.

The past two years were years full of revelations, and self-reflection and I consider myself a better woman for it. I hope it shows in my actions, my parenting, the way I love, and in every book I publish. Enjoy!

Part 1

Chapter One

OLIVIA

Monday, March 30, 2020

Like any other day, I get up with my alarm at seven, get dressed, and head to the kitchen to make my usual pot of coffee. As I wait for it to finish, I reflect on the day ahead. I cannot shake the feeling that something major is about to change in my life. I'm pretty sure it has to do with the one thing I don't want to change — my job. It's hard to admit, but I can't face losing my connection to my sexy billionaire boss, Vincent Jared Taylor III.

As I'm putting creamer in my cup, my phone vibrates with a text. I pick my phone up to check who it is with no real concern because only a limited number of people have this number. However, I see the name, and immediately my heart rate speeds up. That's nothing unusual anymore. It happens every time I think about my boss, and it's even worse when I'm in his presence.

I read the cryptic message he sent, asking me to come to his estate immediately. Now, my heart is speeding for a different reason.

I'd been dreading this day, but I knew it was inevitable. *I'm going to get laid off today, I just know it.* The Coronavirus is finally going to impact me in a meaningful way, and I'll be just another jobless statistic in this crazy mess of a world.

Every day things get worse with this virus. The news is filled with grim numbers — more outbreaks, more fatalities, and more businesses closing. It's changed everyone's lives, and not in a good way. At least the social distancing thing hasn't really bothered me like so many others. My parents always kept me away from people, so even after they passed, I continued to be a loner.

But, even for me, this pandemic has given an entirely new meaning to the word isolation. People are scared to step outside their homes and are constantly afraid of contact with other people. Fear of exposure is paralyzing to some people. The whole world's gone crazy. Between that and the apparent war going on between police and the black community, I don't know what to think. People are tearing whole cities apart — vandalizing, and damaging businesses — and they're so filled with anger. These are bad times.

I really thought I'd escape the hardships of the shutdown because, unlike most employers, mine is filthy rich and is treating this whole thing as a temporary setback. His business is more than able to withstand the rough waters caused by COVID.

I'm not sure what my boss plans on doing to prevent exposing himself and his son to the virus, and it makes me anxious. Could be he plans to lock his mansion doors and stay inside until the pandemic cools down, but where does that leave me? *Unemployed, that's what.*

I've only had this job since the end of 2019 — seven months. Just thinking of the embarrassing circumstances in which we met, and he offered me employment, makes me cringe. It certainly was a fated meeting, and I remember it like it was yesterday...

Chapter Two

OLIVIA

August 2019

I'd just finished an interview at Taylor Industrial, and my dreams had been thoroughly crushed. I walked out of the massive building with my head down in shame and embarrassment.

Ten minutes into my walk home, the skies opened and tried to drown me. I'd forgotten to check the weather report before I left, so I was completely unprepared. Now, not only was I depressed, but I was also completely drenched. Not one cab was in sight, and my phone was dead, so I needed to get out of the rain and find a place to charge my phone so I could get home.

I looked around and my eyes locked on an open sign in the middle of the massive plaza I was passing. The sign was like a beacon, and I ran inside. I was looking anything but pretty at this point — my hair looked like I'd been electrocuted, I had a rip in my tights, and I was soaked through to the skin. I wanted nothing more than to go home, curl up and cry, but first I needed an outlet so I could plug in my phone and then call a ride.

Luckily, my place of refuge was a beautifully decorated coffee shop. Professionally dressed patrons were sitting at tables with their laptops open or chatting on their phones. After being caught in the rain, I resembled a wet dog more than a human. I did not fit in at all.

I shook off my embarrassment and looked around for a restroom. When I saw it, I hurried in and sighed when I saw the wall-mounted hand drier. I maneuvered myself under it and let the warm air blow on my wet clothes. I attempted to fix my hair and failed, so I emerged from the bathroom resigned to the fact that it was just not my day.

The first person I noticed was a beautiful older woman who could only be described as fabulous. I was so busy admiring her that I didn't realize she was heading directly toward me.

"Hello," she said warmly, stopping in front of me.

"Hi," I replied shyly.

"Welcome to Santorini's. My name is Maria. My husband Pedro and I own this fine establishment. I've never seen you in here before, so I thought I'd come and welcome you."

"Thank you. I am so happy I found this place. It's a perfect shelter from the storm."

"The weather is dreadful, isn't it? Well, we're happy to be here for you. Can I get you anything? It's on the house."

"Thank you, I appreciate that. I do have a favor to ask though. Can charge my phone somewhere that's not so...public? I'm kind of a mess."

"Of course. Let's get you some coffee, and I'll show you a good place to do just that. Sound good?"

"Yes, thank you."

"Okay, how do you take your coffee?"

"Hot, French vanilla coffee, lite and sweet would be great."

"Okay, it'll be up in a second," she says, disappearing behind the counter.

True to her word, three minutes later, coffee in hand, I followed her past the other customers and down a hall to a small private conference room.

"Come, señorita. This should be perfect for your needs," she says as she turns on the lights. The space was bigger than the café area, and even more opulent, which was surprising.

"You can sit here, dry off a bit and let your phone charge. If you need me, I'll be out front."

"Thank you, so much. I really appreciate this."

"Everyone needs a little help occasionally. I'm simply paying it forward," Maria says warmly.

"Okay, thank you." She says and I watch her go. As she does, I put my phone on the charger, sit, and immediately my body slumps into the chair, finally able to relax. I lean my head back inadvertently taking slow breaths, and take in this moment of quiet and peace, especially after my day.

As I sit and process today, out of nowhere, I feel a presence and the hairs on the back of my neck stand up. I stand, turn around, and gasp when I see a shadow at the back of the room. I jump up, ready to run, but then the shadow starts speaking.

"Maria usually keeps this room closed this time of day, so when I heard her bring you back, I got curious."

"Oh," I say, hurrying to unplug my phone.

"No, don't feel you have to leave. I'm sorry I disturbed you Ms.—"

"Hunt. Olivia Hunt."

"You can stay here. It's not a problem."

"I just needed a moment alone. I'm fine now, and my phone is charged enough to make a call."

"Why?"

"What do you mean, why?"

"Aside from being caught in the rain with a dead phone, what happened to put you in such a bad mood that drying off and a cup of good coffee can't fix?"

"Oh, I umm, had a job interview and…it didn't go very well. I needed to regroup."

"Oh, I see. Well, I'm sorry that happened."

"Yeah, me too."

"What kind of job was it?"

"Um, you ask a lot of questions for a stranger. Who are you?"

"I'm just a…fan of the coffee here. I'm sorry, I should have introduced myself. I'm Vincent."

"Hi, Vincent. It's nice to meet you," I say as I get ready to bolt out the door.

"Indulge me. What type of job are you looking for?" he asks as he starts walking toward me from the back of the room.

The instant I can see his face clearly, my heart lurches. He's the most beautiful man I've ever seen in real life! He looks like he just stepped out of GQ magazine. The way he carries himself — it just screams power, class, and wealth. I don't belong in the same room as this man.

"Do you need to see my driver's license before you give me an answer?"

"Oh, no. I'm just surprised you care. Anyway, I was applying for an internship at Taylor Industrial, but I wasn't qualified."

"I see. So, what will you do now?"

"I don't know. I'm open to anything right about now."

"I think we can help one another."

"How's that? I'm not into anything shady," I say quickly, wondering where he's going with this.

"Well, I'm a business owner and it just so happens I employ people. You seem to be looking for a job, so..."

"What kind of business do you own?"

"The answer to that question is a bit complicated. Just believe me when I say I have a position for you if you're interested."

"What position?"

"If you're truly interested, I'd like to discuss it with you more formally. Could you come to my office for an interview?"

"You're serious?"

"Yes, I'm serious. This is me offering you a job."

"No offense, but I don't know you. I don't think I should accept your offer."

"I really think you should. Your suspicions will be put to rest once you get to know me," he says, moving closer to me and making my heart rate increase tenfold.

"I don't think I'm really comfortable with your proposition."

"You will be, if you just give it and me a chance."

Now, I'm even more intrigued by his offer than I was before, which can't be good. What's crazy is I believe him, despite not knowing him. Our apparent attraction and the fact that the look he's giving me is making me tingle all over adds to the allure. It does seem like he's serious. Maybe I could work for him.

I suddenly think of this saying that goes something like, "Whatever challenge scares you the most — do it. If there's no risk involved, then more than likely it's not worth it in the first place." This is the exact opposite of the way I've lived my life since my parents died. Maybe it's time for me to take on a challenge that scares me. What he's proposing scares and excites me, so maybe this a risk worth taking.

"All right. I'll meet with you."

"*You surprise me, Olivia Hunt. I expected you to stick with your first answer, but I'm glad you didn't.*"

"*Well, I figured there's no harm in hearing you out. Besides, I'm not sure I'm okay with being so predictable that even a stranger knows what I'll do,*" *I say, and he laughs with a sexy rumble I wouldn't mind hearing daily.*

"*Logical and beautiful, you're quite the surprise, Ms. Hunt. I believe we'll work well together,*" *he says, taking out his wallet. He plucks an engraved card out of it and extending a card to me. "My personal email and cell number are on the back. Email me at this address and then watch for a reply from my assistant, Veronica. She'll give you the address." I hesitate a second before taking the card. "I'll expect you at eight o'clock sharp tomorrow morning,*" *he said as put his wallet back in his pocket.*

"*Now that that's solved, and since you're not my employee yet, I can't resist.*"

"*Resist wha—*"

His mouth came down on mine, silencing my question. He puts his hand behind my head and pulls me closer, and I just melt into him. The kiss deepens and I nearly lost myself when his phone rings and breaks the spell. He steps back and answers, his eyes never leaving mine.

"*What is it, Veronica?*" *he asks, as he licks his lips and continues to stare at me.*

"*Fine. I'm on my way,*" *he says, sounding irritated.*

"*I'm sorry, work calls. Do me a favor?*"

"*Mm-hmm.*"

"*Don't change your mind. Things happen for a reason. Forget about what just happened, the job offer is legitimate. Don't worry, once you're working for me, that won't happen again.*"

"Okay," I say, dazedly, still floating on the euphoric feeling from my very first kiss.

"You've made my day, Ms. Hunt. I look forward to our meeting in the morning."

The following morning, I finally knew why the address on the card looked familiar to me — I was summarily rejected here the day before. I really hope fate isn't playing a mean trick on me. I don't want a repeat of yesterday.

I walk into the massive building with no small amount of trepidation. I ride the elevator to the correct floor and follow the instructions his assistant sent me. I end up in front of a door marked "VINCENT JARED TAYLOR III, CEO". What?!

Chapter Three

OLIVIA

I can't help but smile as I think about it now, that CEO placard really threw me for a loop!

Yes, the chain of events that led to me working for my sexy, billionaire boss is like something from a book, dream, or movie. He was right, meeting him did happen for a reason and I don't regret any of it. The offer he made that day wasn't what I expected — it was better.

The only disappointing thing about my job is my boss kept his word about never kissing me again. He doesn't even look at me the way he did that day, and I hate it. I loved how he made me feel— like a desirable woman, and without the shame. To have a man like him look and touch me like that for even a second, had to be the highlight of my existence.

I'm learning to live with the loss though. I should've known a man like him would never look twice at me. I genuinely love my job though, which is why I dread the thought of it ending abruptly because of the pandemic.

I have to force myself to get ready to go to this meeting today. I don't want my job to evaporate into thin air. I try to shake the negative thoughts while I get dressed and call an Uber.

I can't stop thinking about worst-case scenarios as the car ride hurtles me closer and closer to my fate. I don't know what will happen to me if I lose this job. I need it to survive and finding a new job in the middle of a pandemic will not be easy.

As we pull up to the usually busy estate, I realize it looks like a ghost town today. I don't see anyone — even the security guard at the gate was missing and the gates were standing open. That's never happened before, making my panic rise a notch higher.

The driver pulls to a stop, and I thank him as I get out. The feeling of dread nearly crushes me as I walk up the steps to the front door. As I lift my hand to ring the doorbell, the door opens and there stands my sexy, forbidden boss.

"Ms. Hunt, thank you for coming on such short notice. Come in," he says as he steps back to usher me into the foyer.

I love walking into this house, it's normally one of my favorite things to do when I start my workday. The entryway is straight out of a movie, and it fills me with wonder. I still can't believe I work here.

"It's beautiful, isn't it?" he asks, and I nearly jump out of my skin.

How the hell did he get so close without me noticing? He smells so good. I swear I'd know his cologne anywhere. "This is my favorite room," I say awkwardly.

"Mine, too."

"I can't stand the suspense, sir. Why did you need to speak to me?" I blurt out, the fear robbing me of the ability to make polite conversation.

"Let's talk in my office," he says with a nod of his head, implying I should follow him.

As soon as we get to his office, I take a seat in front of his massive desk and wring my hands anxiously. I've never been fired before. When seconds go by and he's said nothing, I decide to break the ice. "Have I done something wrong, Mr. Taylor?"

"Of course not. You've been an excellent employee from the moment you started. Okay?"

"Okay…"

"However, I am taking precautions and transitioning everyone to working from home until the pandemic is over. I'll be working from home too. I don't want any of my employees to risk getting sick, and I don't want to risk it either."

"I understand. Thank you for the opportunity," I say with true sadness. "I've really enjoyed working here. Could you provide me with references so I can find a new job quickly?" *Well, I guess I won't be enrolling in those painting classes.*

"You misunderstand, Ms. Hunt. I'm not firing you. I didn't ask you here to fire you, Ms. Hunt. I want to offer you another position here. If you don't accept, I'll understand, and your existing job will be waiting for you when the COVID threat has passed, I give my word on that. So far, are we on the same page?"

"Yes."

"Okay. The position that I want to offer you is full–time and due to the pandemic, live-in. That is non–negotiable."

"I'm sorry, live-in? Do you mean you want me to work and live *here*? In *this* house?"

"Yes, that's exactly what I mean."

"I have an apartment."

"I'm aware, but I can't risk exposure for me, you, and Junior. I'm sure adjustments will have to be made, but anyone having a position requiring them to come into the house or be on the grounds, will be required to take mandatory tests weekly. To avoid that, you can just stay with us. Consider it a quarantine."

"What about my apartment though?"

"When are you scheduled to renew?"

"Uuh, it's a month-to-month lease," I say nervously, all too aware that this can't happen.

"Perfect. What's the problem then?"

"What about my furniture, clothes, and belongings?"

"I can have a moving company at your apartment within the hour and they'll do all the packing. There's no need for you to go back and possibly be exposed. I'll rent a storage unit and put everything you don't need in there. That way you can have it back once this is over. Don't worry about it, I'll take care of everything."

After a long pause, I ask, "If I agree, where will I be staying?"

"There are lots of unused bedroom suites in this house. You can choose whichever one you like. They're all large, but if you need more space, I'm sure we can work something out."

Why am I imagining this job will mean I have to wear a sexy housekeeper costume and killer high heels and walk around with a big feather duster? I feel myself blush. I never got indecent thoughts before I met Vincent, so I'm not sure what to do with the feelings they generate.

"Are you still with me, Ms. Hunt?"

Stop drooling over your boss — either accept the offer or go home. "Yes, sorry. I'm just a little overwhelmed."

"I understand."

"Can you tell me about the position?"

"Well, I wouldn't know what specific title to give it seeing as you will be filling several additional responsibilities you did not have prior to this.

"You'll be the housekeeper and nanny — basically our go-to for everything except for education. This means you'll basically do your usual housekeeper duties, but you'll take care of all needs that may arise for Junior. You'll make all his meals, do his laundry, clean his room, and keep him occupied while I work. As I said, education is not a role I expect you to fulfill because Junior has proven to be a bit… more advanced than kids his age. So, you don't have to worry about that. I understand I'm asking a lot from you out of the blue, but I promise you'll be handsomely compensated. Your salary will be raised to one hundred thousand, annually. Is this agreeable to you?" He asks, and I just stare at him, completely speechless.

Shit! Am I crazy or did he just say I'll make 100K for watching his son, cooking a few meals, and doing laundry?

"Is this real?"

"I assure you, this pandemic, Covid, and this offer are very real. The question is, do you accept?"

Holy Shit! This is real, he's not firing me, he's promoting me. One hundred thousand dollars! I have to take it, right? Wait, something's not right.

"Why me? Why am I the one who gets this offer? Surely you have other employees who would love the opportunity and have been here longer."

"Well… I've seen you interact with Junior, and he genuinely likes you. That's important since he hasn't had a constant female influence in his life before you came along. All the other employees I would trust enough to put into this position are older and they have outside commitments — boyfriends, wives, husbands, kids, etc. You're single, so I thought you'd be a good fit."

At least he's honest. It doesn't feel great to know that the only reason I'm a good fit is that I'm alone in the world.

My face must've betrayed my thoughts, because he quickly adds, "I didn't mean to insult you, Ms. Hunt. I'd be honored to have you here. Do you think this will work for you?"

"I'm not insulted, and I accept. I can do the job."

"Great! I just need to know what you'd like your off days to be."

"Um, we can keep it at weekends."

"Okay, then. Great. Well, I'll call the movers and they'll get there and get started. Do you have a spare key hidden somewhere at your apartment?"

"Yes, there's one under the flowerpot on the front step."

"Great. There are just a few more things." He says as he comes around the desk, leans onto it, and regards me. "Look, these certainly aren't exactly *conventional* circumstances, so I think it's best we just drop the formalities. I want you to be comfortable here since this will be your home for the foreseeable future. When you are home, you should feel free to be yourself. You're not just an employee now, you're a member of the household. So, from now on, I'm Vincent and you're Olivia. Okay?" *Like I could ever feel comfortable in this ivory castle.*

"I'm not sure I can do that."

"Why not? Is it so hard to think of me as someone other than your boss? You did, once." He says.

"I did, but now..."

"Now, what?"

"Well, you can be intimidating to small people like me, that's all. You exist somewhere up in the stratosphere, and I'm here on the ground."

"Well, hopefully as you get to know me, you'll realize that I'm not in the stratosphere, and my feet are firmly on the ground here, with you, Olivia."

"We'll see. I will try my best to honor the request…Vincent." I say as I start making my way toward the door.

"That's all I ask. Which room do you want?"

"The west wing with the natural light. On my off days, it'll be great for painting, and sketching."

"I'd love to see some of your work. Maybe you can help liven this place up with some of your paintings?"

"Really?" I ask, my disbelief at the suggestion apparent.

"Yes, I'd love to have some Olivia Hunt originals hanging on the walls."

"I'd like that, too."

"Great. I won't keep you any longer. I know you're probably dying to go break in your new living quarters. So, before you go, this is yours." He says as he retrieves what looks to be a black card out of his pocket. I don't immediately take it, and I stare at it as if it might bite me. "What's this for?"

"Anything you need. It's my AmEx credit card. I set you up as an authorized user on this account so you can use this."

"What would I need this for?" I ask, my voice filled with horror and panic at what this could imply.

"For work, incidentals, whatever. I know you're filling a new role, and you'll need things. I want you to have everything you need, so I got the card for you in case I am unavailable when you need something."

"So, it's like a company card?"

"Sort of, though you won't have to fill out an expense report or have a limit on spending. You can also use it for personal things. Buy anything you need or want. Money isn't exactly a problem for me, so this is just another perk you get for agreeing to do this job. Consider it an unlimited bonus. It's like Usher said, '*No limit*.'" He's laughing, but I don't think it's funny at all.

This is how it starts. This is how a good girl loses her soul, I think in a panic. "That's generous of you, but I can't. I'd prefer to just come to you directly for whatever supplies, incidentals, or needs that may arise if that's okay with you."

"If that will make you more comfortable, then yes.

"Thank you. Okay, well, I will go to… my room." I say as I gather my purse up, stand, and walk to the door, but he beats me to it. We both simultaneously reach for the doorknob at the same time, and the moment our hands touch, I pull it back as if I had been burned.

It was like *being zapped by a lightning bolt. I can't even look him in the eyes for fear of what my face will reveal.* The sudden butterflies fluttering around in my stomach are no help at all.

"Sorry, see you later." I manage as I brush past him all but bolting out of his presence.

Chapter Four

VINCENT

I was both impressed and shocked by Olivia's reaction. She's usually quiet and almost subservient. I like that she had the backbone to ask me why I chose her for the job.

Olivia is an exemplary employee, and Junior adores her. She's a kind gentle woman, and she renews my hope daily that I made the right choice in hiring her, and that whatever trouble she's in does not involve me, my money, or my company. Her reaction to the black AmEx just now proves that.

My beautiful little housekeeper is an enigma, but I still feel a connection to her that I've never felt with any other woman before. Yes, the anonymity factor I liked so much is gone now, and she's intimidated by who I am, we will get past it. I don't know how, but I know. I'm convinced our fate was sealed from the moment I laid my eyes on her. It felt as if my entire life had been leading up to the moment I met her, and I wouldn't change it. She needed me, the man then, and she needs me now, even if she doesn't know it.

The truth is, after meeting her, I was curious and wanted to know why she was turned away. So, I had all her submitted information sent to me, and I reviewed it.

I found out that she was not qualified for the position because of her lack of a degree in architecture or related field, in-depth knowledge of 3D modeling software such as Autodesk, and Auto-CAD, and hand drafting skills. However, those things she could get. It was something else that made her unemployable for us.

Olivia provided all the same information as the other candidates: original birth certificate, social security number, etc. She looked entirely legit on the surface, but upon inspection by our Legal and HR specialists, it was discovered that something was off.

After a careful inspection, they reported all her documents as high-level forgeries. When I asked them to explain to me how they came to that conclusion, they gave me a crash course on all the telltale signs of forgeries and told me about the markers present on her documents. Turns out, the only thing legitimate about Olivia Hunt was her GED.

This news rocked me. I couldn't reconcile the innocent woman I met, and the very fake, potentially criminal life she was leading. She's so transparent that I can almost always tell everything she's thinking and feeling by watching the expressions on her face. How can someone like that be living a lie? Is it possible she doesn't know she's living a lie?

Regardless of the mystery, Ms. Hunt was and still is much too intriguing for me to let get away. That's why I created this position for her, but not before hiring a PI to find out everything about her. I'm positive she's not dangerous, and I didn't see the harm in satisfying my insatiable curiosity.

To date, they've come up with nothing which is frustrating. I don't know what it is, but I know there's something going on. Even though I have confidence that her past and her employment with me have nothing to do with one another, I have no intentions of stopping my investigation.

Unfortunately for me, I haven't had another glimpse of that passionate woman from the day we met, but I still have hope she's there under the surface. I can't make the first move because I gave her my word I wouldn't — and I always keep my word.

If something else happens between us, it'll have to be initiated by her. No, I'm still not comfortable pursuing a relationship while she's my employee, but I want her with every fiber of my being, and I can't fight it anymore. At this point, I'm not able to distinguish whether my desire for her is really for her, because she's forbidden to me, or if it's something more.

Aside from Olivia, I've only felt this way about a woman one time in my life — with Lauren Cavendish, Junior's mom. That whole relationship turned out to be a disaster, and it left me wary of all women and relationships. No one likes to be used for their money and connections, and that's exactly what Lauren did. She didn't love me — hell, I don't think she even liked me — she was just a great actress. She made me a pussy - whipped, fool, and I refuse to be with anyone like her ever again. At least I got Junior out of it. I still don't understand how a mother could give up her child like that — yet I'm glad she did. Junior and I are both better off not having her in our lives.

Sometimes, I need to remind myself that though Olivia has secrets, she's not Lauren. In fact, they're complete opposites — where Lauren was cold, calculating, and deceptive, Olivia is genuine and warm. Without even trying, Olivia has filled a void in Junior's life, and mine too, if I'm honest.

I consciously stop thinking about anything to do with Lauren and get down to the business of getting Olivia moved in. I smile to myself as I end the call with the movers. Call me cocky, but I somehow knew she would stay.

I just hope her choice has more to do with me than the deal I offered her. I saw how curious she was about how this will all work out, but the answers to those unasked questions might just send her running in the opposite direction. *Better leave things as they are, at least for now,* I caution myself.

I sit and think about how challenging it will be to live with the temptation of her twenty- four hours, seven days a week, and I wince. I'll be rocking blue balls for the foreseeable future.

I want her and when I want something, I go for it aggressively. However, I can't do that with her because it will undoubtedly send her running in the opposite direction. That means if I don't want to lose her, I'm going to have to practice something I am not accustomed to, patience.

Shit, I need to get out of my head. I get up, stretch, and go to check in on Junior. When I get to the door of his room, I overhear him and ask Olivia a question.

"Olivia, do you talk to your mom?" Junior asks innocently.

"No, she's gone."

"Do you miss her?"

"Sometimes."

"I never had a mom. What's it like?"

"I think my mom was a bit different from other moms, but do you know what I know about dads from watching yours."

"What?"

"Well, dads are cool. They dress up and go to work, but they also spend as much time with you as they can, because they love you. They like to pick you up, tickle you, and chase you around the yard. They watch movies and do sports with you. They teach you right from wrong and how to be kind. Does that describe what it's like with your dad?"

"Yeah, but it would be nice to have a mom too."

"I'm sure it would be, and it's okay if you want that. But, I also think it's important to appreciate the parent you have. Right?"

I'm amazed and a little relieved when he nods his head yes.

Seeing them together and hearing the advice she gives him, I can't help but smile. There are a lot of mysteries about this woman, but her character is not in question. I'm glad I followed my instincts and asked her to move in. Junior has never bonded with any of the women I've introduced him to over the years until now, even though he obviously longs for a female influence in his life.

When I told him about my pandemic avoidance plan, he was happier than I've ever seen him. Until that moment, I don't think I truly realized what he was missing in his life — a mother figure.

I decide to leave them to their conversation, and head to my bedroom to think. I've got some free time, which is a treat I rarely give myself. Being a dad and the CEO of a huge corporation usually takes up all my time. I think I'll indulge in another treat that's even rarer than a day off — a nap. I know I'll sleep peacefully because Olivia is here to take care of things.

***

I wake up an hour later and come downstairs just as the movers pull up in front of the house. I watch from the window as Olivia goes out to greet them. The driver gets out and walks up to her, wearing a flirtatious smile. I immediately don't like him. I grab my shoes, stuff my feet into them and head outside.

I don't normally feel territorial or jealous, but right now all I want to do is punch that guy right in his smiling face. As I get closer, I can tell just by looking — this guy is a loser. *She's going to be mine and he needs to back the fuck off!*

I make it outside in record time, and I approach them in seconds. "Olivia, Junior's looking for you. I can handle everything from here." I say, lying through my teeth to interrupt their conversation. She turns to look at me, and the smile she's wearing goes away instantly.

Shit, maybe my tone was a bit sharper than I realized. I smile at her in what I hope is a reassuring way.

"See you later, *Olivia*." He says, as she walks away. "Damn, that is a sweet piece of ass." He says, finally taking his eyes off her. Out of my peripheral, I see her stop and turn at his statement, telling me she heard him. That only makes it harder for me to refrain from punching him in his smiling fucking face.

When she's out of hearing range, I turn and snap, "How about you start doing your job, now." I say, wishing he'd give me one reason to deck him.

"Are you her boyfriend or something?"

"I'm her boss as well as the man signing the checks. That means, for all intents and purposes, I'm your boss today, too. So, do the fucking job I'm paying you for and leave."

"Oooh, I get it, I'm stepping on your territory, huh *boss*?" he taunts, giving me a big lascivious wink.

"You willing to lose your job to get the answer?"

"Nah, you got it, *boss*. Besides, I get your anger. If I had a fine piece of ass like that working for me, I'd walk around with blue balls and a shitty attitude, too. I wouldn't bother though, she's probably a terrible lay, and she looks like the clingy type. I can try her out, and get back to you if you want, *boss*."

The next few seconds are a blur. All I know is one minute he was talking, and the next he was on the ground bleeding, holding what I suspect to be a broken nose, and my hand is throbbing.

His co-worker watches as he rolls around on the ground shakes his head and goes back to work. I walk over to him and address him directly.

"What's your name?"

"Jeremy, sir."

"Well Jeremy, if you can get everything loaded into the house, and take the remaining furniture to a storage unit on 43rd Street without that idiot's help, I'll pay you two grand in addition to whatever you are being paid hourly from your company."

"I can do that, no problem." He says and goes right back to work.

I walk over and look down at the dumb ass who's still rolling around on the ground yelling expletives. "Going forward, here's a tip; You don't bite the hand that feeds you. You're fired, now get the fuck off my property."

"Fuck you! That was assault!"

"Have your lawyer contact my lawyer when you get the police report filed. Now, I'll say it one more time, and then I won't be *saying* anything else. Get the *fuck* off my property!" I say as I watch him get up and walk down the driveway.

When he's out of sight, I get Jeremy's bank details before I start walking back up to the house.

I look up just in time to see Olivia in the window, staring at me with wide eyes. *Fuck, she saw the whole thing.*

Well, this is turning out to be a very annoying day.

Chapter Five

VINCENT

I care very little about what people think of me, except for Pops, my grandfather who raised me, Junior, and now Olivia.

The advice and opinion I value especially is that of Pops. That man is the reason I am who I am today. Pops has been a constant role model and he's the father of my heart, my everything.

I was home-schooled from a very young age by the best of the best, therefore I was advanced, so I didn't have an ordinary schedule. I used to live to get up and go to work with him every day. As I got older and started showing interest in the business, he began teaching me how to look, dress, and be the image of the quintessential business executive. It wasn't unusual for me to sit in on the meetings and conferences, or fly out with him to meet with manufacturers, suppliers, and even investors. I'm not the Vincent Parker he expected to carry on his legacy, however, I'm the son he trusts to do so, and I take extreme pride in this fact.

I need to repair the damage I did with Olivia today, and it's time to call in the big dog to help me. So, I pull up his contact and place the call. He picks up on the first ring, like usual. "Hey, Pops."

"Hey, son. How are you?"

"I'm okay. When are you coming for a visit?" I ask, avoiding what I really want to talk about.

"Cut the shit. You didn't call me to ask when I'm coming to visit. What's wrong?"

I've never been able to get anything past Pops. I swear he has a sixth sense when it comes to me. However, at this moment, I appreciate the fact that he always has a solution to whatever problem I'm having.

I'd already filled Pops in on how I met Olivia, so I give him a rundown of today's events, ending with me punching the mover.

"Can I ask you something?" I asked after I finished my recap.

"Sure."

"How did you feel when you first met Gram?"

"Hell, I felt the earth shake, the sky fall, and the universe shift. She was so beautiful, and her energy was so magnetic and ethereal. I knew she'd be mine because I wouldn't have it any other way."

His response brought an immediate smile to my face because it was exactly how I felt when I saw Olivia.

"Sound familiar?" he asks.

Of course, it sounds familiar, I thought, but remained silent.

"Look, you don't let go of a woman like that, son. Trust me, you'll regret it if you do. I know Lauren did a number on you, but not all women are like her. This new gal may just be the one to show you that. I certainly hope so. I'd love nothing more than to see you settled and happy. Life is short, you have to make it count while you can. Put a little effort in it — woo her, seduce her, and win her heart, son."

"I just don't know where to start."

"Well, let's talk this out," he says with confidence.

We put our heads together, and an hour later, I had a plan.

Chapter Six

VINCENT

Looks like yet another restless night for me. Olivia is still avoiding me, so every night I walk past her door, hoping I'll run into her so we can talk. I fucked up when I punched that guy. The look that I saw in her eyes that day still haunts me.

Pops thinks I bruised her pride and then treated her like property. She obviously didn't like my little testosterone show, so he's probably right. *Wow, I can really be a jerk sometimes!* I'm going to do what he recommended and give her space, but it's not easy when she's right here all the time.

Being the idiot I am, I stop at her door and listen. Tonight is no different from every other night this week, but I still listen for a few minutes anyway. I can't help but resent the fact that she sleeps like a baby, while I can barely sleep at all. I'm a ticking time bomb, and my balls are so blue I'm surprised they're not glowing.

As I start to walk away, I hear a muffled sound. I stop and wait for a few beats. When I hear nothing, I start walking away again, shaking my head in disgust at how pathetic I am. I take two steps, then hear it again. So, I go back to the door and listen. *Is she okay? Should I go check?*

"Yes!" I suddenly hear Olivia moan through the door, and I feel my blood heat.

That was definitely a moan. What the hell is going on in there? Is there someone in there with her? Wait, that's impossible. This is Olivia who blushes and scurries away whenever I get close to her. She would never bring a man here. I suddenly realize these jealous, insecure feelings are what got me into my current predicament.

"Oh!" I hear. *Okay, fuck this. I'm going in. I need to know what's going on in there.* I turn the knob, slowly open the door a bit, and look around the room. The full moon's light is coming in through the window and I can see the room clearly. When I'm sure no one else is here, I look back at the bed, and my dick hardens instantly.

My sweet little Olivia sleeps naked! The sheet is wrapped around her feet at the end of the bed. *God, that body...*

"Yes, Vincent!" she moans.

Wait, what? Did she just say my name? I've wanted to hear her say my name just like that since I met her

"Don't stop! Please, Vincent!" she says as she squirms. My dick is so hard that I'm surprised my pants haven't ripped. She's dreaming about me! More than anything, I want to give her the real thing.

She's so beautiful, I think as my eyes roam from her face to her full, beautiful breasts. Her nipples are hard, and all I want to do is bend down and swipe my tongue around the closest one. I just know her response would be everything I want and more. But this isn't the time.

Chapter Seven

OLIVIA

I've never felt like this before. Shy, timid Olivia is gone, and I want him to see all of me. I kick the sheet to the foot of the bed, showing him I'm naked, and his eyes devour me. I smile and crook my finger to beckon him closer, and he slowly crawls onto the bed. He's just inches from me now, and not touching him is torture. Smiling, Vincent covers me in sweet kisses, igniting my skin everywhere his lips touch me.

His hands caress my neck, then travel slowly down to my breasts. It's sweet agony. His kisses follow his hands, and I gasp as he reaches my nipple, and it hardens with the touch of his hot tongue. I arch into him, begging him to give me more, of what, I'm not sure. I just know I need more.

I moan as he nips at my tender skin, and his rumbling laugh vibrates my skin and makes me cling to him. His lips are on the move again, and he kisses a trail downward. He's going too far, and I try to stop him, but I can tell he knows I don't really mean it. He reaches my forbidden place, and I'm overcome by desire. I can't *help it, I moan again. The sound turns him into a madman, and a wave of euphoria hits me as he swipes his tongue between my folds.*

His tongue is doing magical things to me, and I can feel the tension building inside me. I want more. I arch my back and open myself to him. "Yes, Vincent! Yes!" I scream before my body goes rigid and wave after wave of the most amazing feelings passes through me.

My eyes pop open and my body feels boneless and feverish. I'm disoriented, but then I remember the dream. *Where did those wicked thoughts come from?* I can hear my mother's voice in my head, speaking in that sanctimonious tone she always used when she wanted to shame me, *"I always knew it. You're a whore! Only whores have thoughts like those."*

Chapter Eight

POPS

Quintana Roo

I end the call with Vincent, and I'm wearing a huge smile. If I'm right, my grandson is in love, and can't tell his ass from his face right now. He's in deep. I hope this nice girl will show him that a relationship can be something other than misery. He needs that. When he found out Lauren didn't love him, the light in his eyes went out and it never really came back. I know he loves Junior more than anything, but he needs to open himself up so he can find romance too.

Vincent needs to stop thinking that women only want him for his money and power. I was lucky to find a wonderful woman the first time around. I just regret that I helped to make him the cynic he is today by drumming it into his head that women like his grandmother are a rare commodity. I think I gave him the idea that he could never find someone like that for himself.

I'm not much better. I didn't think it was possible to experience that type of love twice in my lifetime, however, I was wrong.

After my wife died, I decided my only role other than CEO was to be Vincent's parent. I thought I could be happy being alone. Then, one day I bumped into Patricia Lawson.

I met her in the company's human resources office, and my life changed forever. I overheard her talking to our HR director and realized she was quitting. I hate to lose people, so I interrupted and asked why she was leaving.

She looked up at me and I felt like I'd been tazed! All I could do was stare at her in shock as she told me that her former boss, Mr. Richardson, had quit, and she felt like there was no longer a place for her in Taylor Industrial.

Once she said that I remembered her. She *was* Michael Richardson's quiet, frumpy executive assistant; however, she's changed. She looked softer and more feminine, and she seemed to have lost some weight. Gone was the woman in shapeless big, old lady clothes, with big hair, and bushy eyebrows. In her place was a sexy woman in a power suit that outlined a curvy body, with a pixie cut framing an oval-shaped face with striking hazel eyes.

I didn't know it, but I was taken aback by the arousal, and the need to know this woman.

"I'm in need of an EA. Are you interested?"

"You want me to be your new EA?" she asked, surprised.

"I do, yes."

"You haven't interviewed me or seen my resume."

"You worked well with Richardson, I don't need to see anything else, Ms. Lawson."

"Fair enough. When can I start?" she asks, and I smile. I like her.

"You don't want a few days off first?"

"I don't know what I'd do with time off. I'm sure my cat has more important things to do than watch me drink wine and watch *The Imitation of Life* on TV."

I was enchanted. "Okay then. I'll see you tomorrow. It was a pleasure to meet you, Ms. Lawson."

"You as well, Mr. Taylor," I say. The truth is, I was hooked at hello.

I can't help but smile as I reminisce about our first year together. We worked in complete harmony. Months after hiring her, Patricia proved to be everything I'd been missing professionally and personally, and we quickly became friends.

Like me, Patricia married young and had been a widow almost as long as I have, however, unlike me, she had hopes of love again. Apparently, that's what motivated her big transformation.

She'd made peace with her husband's death, and for years she chose to bury herself in work to avoid feeling lonely. Over time, our relationship grew into something more than just friendship.

There were just three very big problems. One was my inability to fight my increasing guilt for betraying my deceased wife by even considering a serious relationship with someone else. Two, I promised my late wife in the event of her death, I'd never marry again, and I'm a man of my word.

Three, I worried then and now that Vincent wouldn't approve, and he'd lose respect for me. I'd fallen in love with my EA fifteen years younger than me, and I'd done it on company time. I've always given my all to this business and I dropped the ball. So, I took the coward's way out — I retired ahead of schedule and went into hiding with my lover.

Almost a full two years after that life-changing move, and I'm still hiding. Patricia and I are together, but no one knows. All this time has passed now, and I've selfishly kept her with me, monopolized her time and heart knowing it's time she could have had with someone else who can give her what she wants the most — marriage. In doing so, I've lost her, nevertheless. She's distant, sad, and nothing like the woman I've come to love and adore.

Presently, my biggest fear is what I'll do when, not if she asks me once more to do the right thing by her. I know that this time will be the last, she will leave, and I'll be alone and empty again.

***

"Do you have a minute?" she asks, stepping out onto the patio with me.

"For you, always," I say as we head to the loveseat near the pool. She looks down at her hands as they rest in her lap, and instantly, I know what's coming. She looks so miserable; I can't stand it. I reach over, squeeze her icy-cold hands, and say, "It's okay, Patricia, say what you need to say."

"It's time."

"That's not all you want to say. Say it all."

"I know you're worried about what Vincent will think about us, and I know how important he is to you, but this has gone on too long, Vincent. We are too old to be hiding from your grandson, and I can't do it anymore. I foolishly hoped you asking for the time that you'd have a change of heart, but I suspect it was to assuage me. Today is the day you decide — either you tell Vincent about us and marry me, or you lose me."

"I can't, I just need," I say, knowing it wouldn't matter.

"Don't say time because you've had time — two years," she says as she stands up to go.

I panic and follow her. "Wait! Please, sit back down. Let's talk about this. Please?" I plead.

"I'm not getting any younger, and neither are you. If you can't do this for me, then you don't love me as much as you say, and it's time for me to live my life to the fullest instead of hiding with you." She says. I say nothing because I can't: she's right. I don't deserve her.

"Your silence is my answer. I hope you and your pride will be happy together. I wish you the best, I really do, Vincent. Good-bye." she says as she starts to walk out of my life.

She stops at the doorway and without turning around says, "I'm booking a one-way flight home tonight. I'll send for my things. Please don't contact me. And don't worry, I'll be discreet. No one will ever know we were together."

With that, she disappears from my life, and all I can think is, *Oh, God. It's really over.*

Chapter Nine

POPS

Days after Patricia left, I dragged myself out of bed in time to see the mailman making his way down the street to my mailbox. Deciding I need to go outside at some point, I force myself to go get the mail. I haven't checked it in a while, so I'm not surprised to see a mountain of mail when I open the box.

As the mailman approaches, I start sorting through it. I stop when I come to a strange-looking letter from the states. *Besides Vincent, who the hell knows my address here?* I wonder. I don't remember telling anyone else, other than Patricia, where I am. I'm almost positive it's not from her.

My heart aches whenever I think of her. I can't blame her for leaving. It's all my fault. I snap out of my pity party and open the letter reads:

I know your secret. I'm willing to keep it to myself if you pay me $2 million. You have 24 hours to get the money to me, or I'll start talking.

You know the account number. — L

As the implication of the letter sinks in, I have a stabbing pain in my chest. My last thought before darkness closes in is, *My time has run out in more ways than one.*

Chapter Ten

OLIVIA

I swear this week is dragging slowly, even though living here is downright surreal. I've never slept in a room like this, and I can't believe that I live here. It's a nice feeling, but it can't compare to what I felt last night. Oh, my God, what Vincent did to me in that dream! Even though I've tried to forget it, I don't want to, and I can't stop thinking about it. I've never felt anything like that in my life!

Just the thought of him touching me like he did in that dream has me in a constant state of anticipation because all I want to do is see him, talk to him…touch him. The thought makes me feel a flood of dread and embarrassment. I'm afraid I'm turning into everything my mother said I would, that I'm not a good girl. So, I've been avoiding him at all costs this weekend. Now, it's going to be so much worse after that dream.

The reality compared to the dream, isn't as stimulating to say the least. Nothing like that can happen in real life. He's my boss and good girls don't do that with people they work for. I can hear my mom ranting in my head, "Olivia, being a whore is easy. You have to choose to be a good girl." *But, my God, what Vincent did to me in that dream!* Even though I don't want to, I can't stop thinking about it. I've never felt anything like that in my life!

I need to proceed as if my subconscious never played that scene for me while I slept. I love my job and I don't want to lose it. Also, I don't have a place to live if I quit, because I gave up my apartment when I moved in here. I've just got to play it cool and hope I can keep it together until this quarantine passes.

I look at the clock, realize it's late, and way past time I get my day started. I get up and walk over to the enormous closet that's easily half the size of my old apartment. For whatever reason, I'm not feeling like any of my usual clothes will work today, so I decide to change it up a little by wearing a black workout outfit that's accented with bright blue. I gather the courage to start my day as I get up, brush my teeth, throw my hair up in a bun, and dress.

I head to Junior's room, wake him up, and tell him to wash his face and brush his teeth. While he's doing that, I set clothes out for him, and then head down to the kitchen to make breakfast. My hands shake a little as I look through the fridge for omelet ingredients. I'm pretty sure Vincent will be joining us for breakfast this morning, and I'm not sure how I'm going to handle that.

When I'm done cooking, I head to Vincent's office to tell him breakfast is ready. I approach the slightly ajar door, and I can't help but overhear his conversation.

"That punch was the luckiest thing to happen to that asshole. Tell his lawyer I'll agree to settle for fifty thousand if he signs an NDA. No negotiation. He can either take it or leave it." There's complete silence while the other person speaks, and then I hear him ending the call. I choose that moment to knock on the door.

"Good morning, Olivia," he says cheerfully.

"Hi. Breakfast is ready if you're hungry," I say quickly, feeling guilty for listening in on his call.

"I suppose you heard my side of that phone call?"

"Yeah, sorry about that."

"No need to be sorry. I wasn't exactly being quiet about it."

"I heard the amount you're offering that guy. I feel like it's my fault you're having to pay him so much."

"What would you have to be sorry for?"

"I think you were trying to defend my honor or something, and maybe I overreacted."

"It was worth it, and you didn't overreact, I could have handled it better." he says with sincerity. "Now, let's go eat, I'm starving."

Why would he stick up for me like that? Men like him don't care about the little people. What's his angle? "Give me a few minutes to get the food set out."

"So, have you hired Junior a teacher yet?"

"I have, I interviewed her virtually. Her name is Julia Ellis. She graduated summa cum laude from FAMU in 1991, comes highly recommended. Eventually, she will physically come and teach him on Mondays and Wednesdays and teach him virtually on Tuesdays and Thursdays. However, she will start her first two weeks working virtually while her leg heals from a fall."

"Okay, great. We have time then."

"Time?"

"Yes, I wanted to ask if Junior and I could start a project of sorts; I want to try to set up a classroom for him for when she does come or when she's teaching virtually in one of the rooms. I can paint, and you and him can decorate it together. I think it would be fun and you did say I could liven the place up."

"So, I did." He says, smiling. "That sounds like a great idea."

"Thank you … Vincent," I say as I nervously grab his omelet on his plate. *Why does he have to be so good looking? Hell, what are you thinking? He's your freaking boss. Stop it!*

"Olivia, I can barely string two words together when I'm around you, please don't look at me like that."

Oh, God! Me and my stupid, expressive face. "I'm sorry. How is it I'm looking at you?" I ask, even though I know exactly what he's talking about.

He gives me a look that makes me feel like he can see right through me. All at once, I feel a wave of emotion I can't put words to come over me and all I know is that I need to get away from him. Without a word, I set the plate down in front of him and turn to leave the room.

"Olivia, wait. I'm sorry if I embarrassed you."

"No, I just...I need to find out what's taking Junior so long. He should've been down here by now."

"Olivia, I apologize for being inappropriate. Please, let's just forget about it and have a nice breakfast together."

"I'll send Junior down. I'm sure he wants cereal and I've been teaching him how to be self-sufficient. Please let him get things together for himself. I'm really not hungry, so I'm going to go ahead and start a load of laundry. I'll be back down in a bit to deal with the dishes."

"Okay, I'll let you go for now, but we need to talk later. Just give me five minutes. Okay?"

"Sure," I say, and leave the room as he gets up to pour himself some juice. I give myself a mental shake and head upstairs.

Great, he wants to talk about what happened after Junior goes to bed this evening. *Just what I need,* I think as I turn to the fridge, and pull out the milk and butter. I promised Junior I'd make mac & cheese with his lunch. I grab the Kraft box from the cabinet — I can't believe rich people eat this stuff too — while Junior tells me all about the latest level on Minecraft. Honestly, I'm too distracted to concentrate on what he's saying completely. My head is buzzing with all possible versions of this talk with Vincent, and I haven't found one that doesn't make me want to disappear, immediately.

The afternoon goes by in a blur. Junior is a bundle of energy and I'm exhausted. I usually enjoy the time I spend with Junior, but today it's been like torture. I can't stop worrying about the meeting with Vincent.

Maybe I should make something complicated for dinner. That way my brain will be occupied, and I won't have time to obsess. Cooking for me is a great distraction that helped me get over my anxiety after my parent's untimely deaths.

There's something about following a recipe, and mixing ingredients together that calms me, and it's nice for the moment.

With that in mind, I decide to go all out for tonight's dinner — beef stroganoff complete with homemade noodles, fresh baked bread, and braised red cabbage. And for dessert, my favorite — super-moist brownies topped with vanilla ice cream and homemade caramel sauce.

Just as I'm pulling the pan of brownies out of the oven, Vincent walks in, sniffing the air and smiling.

"Wow, something smells good. I found it hard to concentrate this afternoon with all the mouth-watering smells that kept assaulting me. What exactly have you been doing in here, Olivia?"

"Oh, it's nothing. I just decided we needed something yummy for dinner tonight, so I made my favorites."

"I can't wait to taste *everything*," Vincent says, with a little more enthusiasm than expected.

"Well, it will all be ready in about 10 minutes. If you don't mind, could you and Junior set the table?

"Your wish is my command," he says before walking off to find Junior.

✳✳✳

The meal was a success, and Junior even ate all his cabbage. It was nice to know the effort I put into this meal was appreciated. "I hope you guys saved room for dessert," I say as I get up from the table and return to the kitchen.

I'm greeted by a groan from Vincent and, "Yeah!" from Junior.

I laugh as I put two warm brownies each onto two plates, add ice cream, a drizzle of homemade caramel, and a sprinkle of nuts. "Ta-da!" I say as I set the plates in front of them.

"This is amazing, Olivia. How did you know brownies are my favorite?"

"I didn't, but they're my favorite too."

"I hope you don't plan to cook like this often. Because if you do, they might have to roll us out of here when the pandemic is over," Vincent says, chuckling.

"Don't worry. I won't do this all the time. I just felt like we needed something special, so I cooked. I might've gotten a little carried away though."

"It was just right. I'll just have to work out extra hard to burn all these calories!"

After we all finished the last bites of dessert, Vincent asked Junior to clear the table.

"He doesn't have to do that," I say, quickly standing and grabbing my plate. "It's my job."

"Nonsense. You cooked that amazing meal, so we can thank you by clearing the table. You don't have a problem with that, do you, son?"

"Nope, especially if it means I can have another brownie."

"Okay, Junior. It's a deal."

As Junior entered the kitchen, Vincent leaned over and whispered, "Could you meet me in my office after Junior's asleep?"

"Uh, sure. I'll be there."

"Nothing's wrong, we just need to talk. Remember?"

Yeah, how could I forget? I've been obsessing about it all day! "Okay. I'll be there once I'm sure he's asleep."

An hour and thirty minutes later, I shut Junior's bedroom door and trudge sullenly down the hall to Vincent's office. I try to take as much time as possible to get where I'm going, but I still get there too quickly for my comfort. *He can't fire me now. With all the shutdowns and the pandemic raging, I doubt I can find another job. Plus, I don't have anywhere to live…*

"There you are," Vincent says as he steps out of his office doorway. "I was beginning to think you'd forgotten."

"Sorry, it took a while to get Junior to go to sleep. He was keyed up about another getting to another level in his game, and he had to tell me all about it."

"Yeah, he does get excited about his games. Poor kid, it's the only thing he's got to do for entertainment with us trapped here like we are. Come on in and have a seat. Can I get you a drink?"

"Uh, sure. Whatever you're having is fine."

"You sure about that?"

"I don't want you to go to any trouble."

"Okay, but I'm not sure you know what you're asking for," he says as he pours a little amber liquid into a shot glass.

"Here you go."

"Thanks. So, what did you want to talk to me about?" I ask, deciding to just get it over with. Needing a little courage, I took a gulp of the drink and nearly died. "Ugh, what is this stuff?" I ask when I could get the words out, my throat still burning.

"Sorry, it's called Old Rip Van Winkle. It's pretty much the best aged bourbon there is, but I guess it's an acquired taste."

"Apparently. God, how much did you pay for this stuff?"

Chuckling, he says, "Oh around sixty thousand."

"*What?*" I sputter. "Are you serious?"

"Yes. They only make a few cases each year, and its aged for twenty-five years. It's well worth the price tag."

"We live in very different worlds," I say, still reeling from what he's just said. *Sixty grand for something that tastes like liquid fire, and he's acting like this is normal! I do not belong in this man's world.*

"We also live in the same house, so maybe we should confront the… issue of our attraction." He says just as I began to cough due to my attempt to choke down this overpriced, disgusting, hot liquid.

"You don't have to finish it. I'd never make you do anything you don't want to, Olivia."

"No, I need to figure out what the big deal is about this stuff. Obviously, if people pay that much for it, there must be something I'm missing," I say, taking another cautious sip. This time, it doesn't seem so harsh, and it goes down my throat a little smoother. It still burns, but I can taste something more than alcohol this time — a hint of vanilla and cherry.

Vincent is watching me closely the whole time and smiles a secret smile when he sees I'm starting to get it. "I'm glad to see that you're willing to give things a second chance. Sometimes, first impressions don't give you the full picture."

I look at him, wondering if he's talking about the drink or something else entirely.

"That was definitely better than my first gulp."

"Maybe some things are better when savored slowly, even this very expensive, overpriced drink of mine." He says and the look he gives me makes my panties want to fall off.

Suddenly, my mother is in my head again, yelling, "*Be a good girl and fight your promiscuous urges, Olivia.*"

God, why does she still have such a hold on me, even after all this time? Pushing her out of my mind, I look up at my handsome boss and ask, "Okay…now, back to what you wanted to talk about."

"Our attraction."

"Yes, that."

"Do you know what desire is?" He asks, and I feel it again, the butterflies.

"Not exactly. Before we met, I didn't really interact with men…or a lot of people."

"Okay, so what about me? What would you describe your interactions with me as?"

"Um…. Interesting." *Torturous. Exciting. Intense.*

"That's it?"

"Yep. What about you?"

"Well, I'd say frustrating, especially when you look at me the way you do."

"How do I look at you, exactly?"

"Like you did when I kissed you. Like you want me to do it again. I told you when you became my employee that could not happen again. I never go back on my word, yet every time I'm near you, I feel myself ready to do just that." He says.

Shit! There it is again; racing heart, butterflies, and my panties are now suddenly ... wet. "You're wrong. I don't think about it, or you like that at all."

"You know, you aren't very good at hiding your feelings — they show on your face, as clear as day."

God, I'm going to die of embarrassment. He knows I'm fantasizing about him.

"I just need you to know regardless of the attraction I feel for you, I would never take advantage of my position. Do you understand?"

I just stare at him for a beat, then ask, "No. What exactly do you want from me?"

"I don't really think you can handle that answer just yet."

"Well, why don't you let me know when you figure it out," I say as I stand to leave.

"Don't go yet," he says.

"No, I need to go. This conversation is confusing and uncomfortable, and I'm done with it for now." I say as I turn to head for the door when he grabs my hand.

I turn to look at him, and he looks so ... lost that I can't resist when he pulls me toward him. Chills run down my spine as he encircles me with his arms and pulls me close. It feels wrong, yet it feels like ... home — but I know it's wrong.

"Do you know how beautiful you are?" he says tilting my chin up to meet his gaze as he runs his hand along my cheek.

Instead of feeling cherished by this move, all I feel is bone-deep fear. Fear that what my mother drilled into my head all those years is true — I'm wicked and I'm going to hell. This thought makes me step away. "I can't do this."

"Olivia, you cannot keep running from this, from passion. Talk to me," he implores, not releasing my hand.

"I can't be *this*."

"What do you mean by that?"

"It doesn't matter. I need to go to my room, now." I tell him, pulling away.

"Olivia, I didn't mean to offend you, what I'm trying to say is I just want you to acknowledge that I'm not just your boss, I'm a man Olivia. You are a loving, kind, beautiful, intelligent, woman and we could be good for each other." He says, and I suddenly feel tears sliding down my face. *How could he know that about me when I don't? He can't be serious, right? We'd never work. Why can't he see that?*

Vincent catches a tear with his thumb and as he does, I look into his eyes, and it's impossible to deny the feelings he stirs in me.

"I know you feel it. I feel like this every time I'm around you." He tells me, and I look away from him.

There are just too many secrets between us — all of them mine. We can never be anything more than employer and employee. I need to stop this.

"No, I don't know what you mean, Mr. Taylor," I manage as I step out of his arms, effectively putting physical and verbal distance between us.

"Are you sure?" he asks, staring straight into my soul.

"Y-yes," I stutter, as I avoid his gaze. *He knows I'm lying.*

He abruptly pulls me back into his arms, and tips my head back and kisses me deeply. What I fear the most is the that it feels so good because it is wrong, forbidden to us.

This is hedonism. It's a sin. This is how fallen women are created. This is wrong — stop! My mind screams at me, but my body isn't listening. *What the hell are you doing?* My brain tries again. *You know what giving yourself to a man like him means. You know his type. Only a whore would allow this!* With each chastising thought, my body gets more and more rigid and unresponsive, until Vincent realizes something is wrong.

Stepping away, I say shakily, "I have to go."

"Olivia, we should talk—"

"No, we shouldn't. This can't happen again, or I'll be forced to turn in my resignation if it does. I don't want to do that, but I will."

He just stares at me for a beat, then says, "I understand. I'm sorry."

"You don't need to apologize. It takes two, but this thing has to stop." I say as I walk out the door. I don't stop or look back. I go to my room and close and lock door. My heart is racing. I never imagined sinning would feel like this.

My parents never warned me about how good it felt, they only told me I shouldn't do it. I don't suppose they wanted me to know that whoring could be pleasurable. I'm sure they thought if I knew that I wouldn't be able to help myself.

If I'm being honest with myself, I've been a whore since the day I accepted this position. Vincent tempted me from the beginning and made me want to be sexy and promiscuous. I thought it could be my secret vice — lusting after my boss. — but clearly, I'm not ready for all the things I've been fantasizing about. Now, I'm playing a game that I don't know the rules to.

All I can hope is that moving me in to care for his child to seduce me wasn't his plan from the beginning. That would add a manipulative and controlling factor I couldn't get past. It's time to put the brakes on and stop wanting something that will never be. I need to tread carefully or I'm going to be the one to get hurt.

Now, I have no choice but to stick it out because I'm basically trapped until the virus is controlled. I doubt it would be easy to find a job right now with everything shut down. I just need to keep a low profile, do my job until something better presents itself or the restrictions ease, and maybe I can move out without causing a scene.

I grab my laptop and flop onto my bed. I go to my Indeed. com profile, pull up my resume, and give it a quick once-over before moving on to search for a new job. I need a backup plan quick. Better to hope for the best and prepare for the worst.

Chapter Eleven

VINCENT

It's been two days, and I still feel as if I am walking on eggshells. Every time I'd come into a room; she'd go scurrying away like a frightened little mouse. *I'm such a fucking idiot!* She started painting the classroom, and honestly, I feel amazed every time I walk past it, I feel a mixture of desire and admiration. She really put some thought into this.

I'm starting to think this goes beyond us being boss and employee, and I that I need to figure out what it is. But, how?

Intent on fixing whatever's wrong, I leave my office and head to her room. As I round the corner to her hall, I stop short. Junior's knocking on her door, and I hear her tell him to come in. I stand where I can't be seen and just watch. I can't see or hear much, but whatever was said got them both out of there in a hurry. After they leave, I walk past her room. She didn't shut the door, and her laptop is still on, and indeed is pulled up.

Shit! She's planning to leave! It's time to implement the second part of Pop's plan — seduction.

✳✳✳

Later that evening, I nervously wait for the perfect time to approach Olivia in the laundry room while Junior is asleep. She has headsets in her ears, and I don't want to scare her. She's wearing a sexy in her little purple, yellow, and blue maxi dress that shows a hint of the curves lying beneath. When she turns, I approach slowly as she removes her headsets.

"Hello, Olivia."

"Hi, Mr. Taylor."

"Vincent." I say, persistently.

"No, Mr. Taylor. Is there anything I can help you with?"

"Yes, as a matter of fact. You can stop searching for another job and stop scurrying away like some scared rabbit every time I step into a room."

"I just want to keep my options open in case things do not work out here, and you're right. I've behaved very unprofessionally, I apologize, it won't happen again."

"I know it's been a bit of a weird first week here, so I won't ask how you feel just yet. Instead, I'll ask how you are liking your space."

"I love it, I have no complaints."

"Has it been hard, sleeping somewhere unfamiliar to you?"

"Ugh, no, I've slept okay."

"Just, okay?" I push.

"Yes. Is there anything else I can do for you?"

"Yes, you can answer my question."

"Which is?"

"I just want to know why you're willing to walk away so easily when you love the pay raise, you love the house, you love the room, and you like the kid you take care of. I know it's me, I just don't understand why? Why are you so scared of me?" I ask her as I step into the laundry room.

"Well, it's inappropriate, and I don't know if I like how I feel when you kiss or touch me."

"I don't believe you and neither do you. I do, however, believe that what you do feel for me scares you because you don't have any experience. I have enough for us both, Olivia. I'll be the brave one, you just let me take the lead. Can you do that?" I ask as I close the distance between us. She tries to take a step back, but the dryer is right behind her. There's nowhere for her to go.

"No," she says.

"Why are you scared of this, Olivia?"

"You're my boss. I'm the help, *Mr. Taylor*, and the help doesn't end up with the rich, sexy boss, not in real life."

"You think I'm hot?"

"Is that seriously all you got out of that?" She asks, clearly frustrated.

"You're right, I'm sorry," I say, but she's on a roll and she lets me have it.

"How pathetic do you think I am?! I'm not some model or celebrity. I'm one step away from being a homeless person, and I'm not in your league. I know that, and I've accepted that despite what I or you want. Maybe you've got a hero complex, but I refuse to be your charity case anymore!"

"I never would've guessed it — you're a snob! I thought you were different, but no, you're just like everyone else. I thought maybe you saw the real me, but I guess you don't. If you did, you'd know your bank balance and past don't matter to me. If you'd been paying attention, you'd know I've been tied up in knots from the very first day I met you! I've been trying to get you to admit you feel something, but you can't see past my title to the man. I swear, sometimes I wish I'd never offered you a job!"

"Excuse me, I need to go pack. I don't think I should work here anymore. Thank you for everything but—"

"No, that's not what I meant, I'm sorry. What I meant is I wish I had the balls to ask you out in the first place instead of offering something I knew you wouldn't turn down. I couldn't handle the rejection, and I'm sorry, Olivia. I don't want you to leave. I've been fighting myself over my attraction to you since the day I hired you up until now. Seven months, to be exact. I was *not* looking for a relationship — hell, I don't think I ever would have wanted one again. But, as I've gotten to know you, I realize what I'd lose if I didn't take the risk and tell you how I feel."

"You barely know me. How can you be so sure this isn't just because your lonely, I'm nice to you, and your son likes me? Maybe this attraction will pass."

"You don't know me very well if that's what you think."

"You're right, I don't really know you at all. I'll admit I'm attracted to you, but attraction isn't enough for me to blow up my life."

"Olivia, I was walking by your room your first night here, and I heard you talking in your sleep. You said my name. Not Mr. Taylor, you said Vincent. Apparently, your subconscious doesn't seem to have a problem with us being together. You seemed to really appreciate our "attraction" then. Why is it such an inconvenience now?"

When she says nothing and stares at the floor, I keep going. "Tell me what you're afraid of?" I repeat as I look down into her eyes.

"I'm just afraid of the things you make me want."

"What is it you want, Olivia?"

"You."

"You already have that." I say as I pull her in for a kiss. I put all my feelings and frustration into it as I back her up against the dryer. I keep kissing her as I pick her up, set her on top of the dryer, and step between her legs.

The way she kisses me back, the way she spread her legs wider, and pulls me closer has my dick hard as a rock.

I hook my fingers under the bra and spaghetti straps and pull them down her shoulders to reveal full breasts and rosy nipples. I remove my lips from hers, grab her left breast, and take a nipple into my mouth as I twist and flick her right nipple. Her moans, and the way she leans her head back, thrusting her breasts out to me has me fighting to control.

Just as I'm about to get on my knees and taste that tight, untouched pussy when the sound of the doorbell echoes through the house, breaking the spell.

Fuck! Who the hell's ringing my damn doorbell? No one's supposed to be out running around during lockdown.

"Ugh, I should go get the door, and then I'll start packing," Olivia says, trying to adjust her clothes. Just like that, the wall is back up.

"You're not going anywhere."

"I'm not your prisoner, Vincent. If I want to leave, I can."

"You're absolutely right. But know this, Olivia, you quitting your job doesn't mean this is over. That's a promise."

"Vincent, you know I can never fit into your world! You're better off sticking to the women in your league — it's not me." she says, starting to walk away.

"Olivia, don't walk away yet. Please? You have nowhere else to go right now. You're welcome to stay and continue your employment here. Hear me out, and if you still want nothing to do with me, then I'll leave you alone. Okay?"

"Fine, I'll stay for now and hear you out, but I'm not making any promises."

"That's fair. Now, I'm going to get rid of whoever's at the door."

"Or, since I still work here, *I'll* go get the door."

"No, *we* will get it. You're off the clock." I say, surprising myself when I lace our fingers together and this is your home, too.

"Okay," she says, staring down at our joined hands as we make our way to the door.

This is unusual. Usually, there'd be Steve out there to operate the gate, and announce visitors. Due to pandemic, I had to let the staff go.

I look at the camera as we walk by the security panel, but all I can see is darkness. The porch light is on, so someone is deliberately blocking the camera. *What the hell?* Thinking of Olivia and Junior's safety first, I push her behind me, and swing the door open.

Standing there is the one woman I never wanted to see again, and my temper flares. "What the fuck are *you* doing here?" I demand through clenched teeth.

"That's how you greet the mother of your child?" she asks, clearly enjoying my anger.

"What do you want?"

"Aren't you going to introduce me?"

"Fine. Lauren, this is Olivia. Olivia, this is Junior's egg donor, Lauren."

"Hello," Olivia says quietly.

"Why are you here?" I demand again.

"Well, I'm glad to see that nothing's changed about you," she says, glaring when she notices Olivia and I are holding hands. "Aside from your ... standards." she asks, as she assesses Olivia from head to toe making Olivia flinch, and try to pull her hand away, but I don't let her. There's no way I'm going to let Lauren fuck this up for me.

"Yes, things have changed. I've learned how to recognize soulless leeches, and I now prefer beauty, brains, and heart. Now, you have five seconds to tell me why you're here before I'm slam the door in your face and call the cops," I say shutting her down. No way I'll let a woman like her intimidate Olivia. Olivia is ten times the woman Lauren will ever be.

"I want to see Junior, of course."

"Over my dead body. You gave up all parental rights. Leave or I *will* call the police. I'll have my lawyer get a restraining order against you if you persist."

"I'm his mother. I should be able to see my child."

"In the eyes of the law, you're nothing. The law will agree that you're trespassing. You're not welcome here — ever — so do what you do best and disappear."

"Fine. Is your grandfather available or is he still in Mexico with that pretty little assistant of his? I saw them a while back, and they looked so happy together. Retirement looks good on them," she says, a mischievous expression on her face.

"Get the fuck off my property, Lauren," I say, slamming the door in her face.

Chapter Twelve

POPS

What is that annoying beeping? I wonder as I open my eyes, then immediately slam them back shut against the brightness of the room. I squint and take a look around. *This looks like a hospital room. How'd I get here?* As I mentally try to make sense of my location, a nurse walks in.

"You're awake! I'll be right back; I'm going to page the doctor."

"Wait! What day is it? Where am I?"

"Calm down, sir. You're at Burbank Medical, and it's Thursday. You've been unconscious for three days. You had a heart attack on Monday morning."

"Has anyone called my grandson?"

"No, but now that you're awake I can give him a call if you give me his contact information. I'm sure he's worried about you."

"Thank you, Miss—?"

"Ramos."

"Thank you, Miss Ramos."

"My pleasure. The doctor will be right in to speak with you. Welcome back, Mr. Taylor."

Chapter Thirteen

VINCENT

As I was walking away from slamming the door in Lauren's face, my phone rang. I look down at my Apple watch and see it's an unknown number. Very few people know this number, so I decide I take it without knowing who the caller is. "I'm sorry, Olivia, I need to take this. Will you wait for me?"

"Yeah. I'll be in the living room when you're done."

"Okay," I say as I turn toward my office so I can speak in private. "Hello?"

"May I speak with Vincent Taylor?"

"Speaking."

"Hi, my name is Natalia Ramos. I'm a nurse at Burbank Medical in Burbank, California."

Instantly, I feel a shiver go up my spine and it's difficult to breath. "What's happened?" I ask, trying not to panic.

"Are you related to Vincent Jared Taylor?"

"He— he's, my grandfather. Is he—" I can't bring myself to form the words. Thankfully, I don't have to.

"Don't worry, Mr. Taylor. He's alive, and he's stable. He had a heart attack outside his home on Monday. Are you local?"

"No. I live in Florida. If this happened on Monday, why did you wait so long to call?"

"Your grandfather didn't have any identification on him when he was found, and he's been unconscious since he was admitted. His mailman saw your grandfather clutch his chest and fall to the ground, so he called an ambulance. Your grandfather was lucky, it's hard to tell how long he could have laid there if no one had been around. Hector, the mailman, stopped by after his shift this afternoon to check on your grandfather and he brought your grandfather's mail with him. One letter was from Taylor Industrial, so I researched the company, called, and was transferred to this number."

"Thank you. I appreciate everything you did to track me down."

"There's one more thing, Mr. Taylor."

"Yes?"

"The mailman also gave us the piece of opened mail he found in your grandfather's hand. I can't be certain, but it looks like a blackmail letter. We didn't know if we should turn it over to the police, so we'll give it to you when you get here and you can decide what to do with it."

The minute she said blackmail, Lauren's icy smile came to mind. It was all I could do to contain my rage.

"What did the letter say?" I ask stiffly.

"The letter said, I know your secret. I'm willing to keep it to myself if you pay me $2 million. You have 24 hours to get the money to me, or I'll start talking. There was no signature, just the letter L."

"Thank you for letting me know. I'll deal with it as soon as I get there. Can he have visitors?"

"Yes, he can have visitors, but you may be delayed for several days before you can see him. You must be quarantined and test negative before your scheduled departure. By the time you get here, your grandfather should be able to go home, though he may need someone to help him for a while. It's better for him to leave the hospital and get away from potential COVID-19 exposure. How quickly do you think you can get here? He's already asking for you."

"I'll be there as soon as I'm cleared to leave. I'll be traveling with my son and fiancé."

"I'll let him know."

"Thank you." I end the call and sit there staring. I'm completely stunned. I need more answers. Lauren is good for something, it appears. She let me know that Patricia had been with Pops. So, I look up her number and called.

"Hi, Patricia."

"Vincent, is everything okay?" she asks with concern, and I feel like crying. Nothing is okay.

"No, everything is not okay. Before I tell you what has happened, I need to ask you a question and I need complete honesty from you. Okay?"

"Okay."

"Tell me everything about Quintana Roo." I say and proceed to do just that.

I was genuinely at a loss. I almost can't believe what she is telling me about my Pops. I just can't understand why he didn't tell me.

Considering her honesty, and the obvious heartbreak she was experiencing, I told Patricia what happened. She was clearly missing him, and under the circumstances, I asked her if she wanted to go back with us and she agreed eagerly. I smiled at that because she wouldn't be rushing to his side if she was completely done with him. *Women!*

"Thank you for being so understanding. I'll wait to hear from you regarding the itinerary." She says before disconnecting.

After the call ends, I sit and take a few minutes to get my emotions under control. My head is spinning. I can't believe that Pops retiring early was all bullshit so he could sneak off to live his double life. I just can't wrap my head around it. For the first time in my life, I feel like I don't know Pops at all. I never thought that was possible.

I push those thoughts away for now. I have to make travel plans and have Lawrence deal with Lauren. Pops had a heart attack because of her blackmail scheme, and she's going to pay for it.

I head down to the living room to find Olivia and stop in my tracks when I hear voices.

"I do. I just like to give people a chance to be good. That's one of the many differences between you and me," I hear Olivia say.

"No need to be so self-righteous. I'm just saying, you're a little nobody, and he's a fucking Taylor, for God's sake. The minute he gets tired of you—"

"Get the fuck out of my house!" I yell as I walk into the room. "I thought slamming the door in your face would give you the hint that you're not welcome here."

"Oh, don't be so dramatic. Olivia was just being polite, unlike you. She let me in so we could have a little talk."

"Oh, really? You're going to play all innocent now? I know you sent a letter to Pops trying to blackmail him!"

"I don't know what you mean."

"Oh, knock it off. I know it was you. What kind of woman blackmails an old man? He never said a word against you when we were together, or after. What the fuck is wrong with you?"

"Oh, please. Two million is nothing to a man like him, or you."

"Then why the fuck did your blackmail letter give him a heart attack?"

"I imagine *Pops* has many secrets, and any one of those could have been the reason for his incident."

"Let me make myself clear. By morning, I'll have a restraining order against you. You won't get a single penny from this family. If you come near any of us again, I will make you wish you hadn't. Understand?"

"We'll see about that," she says, shoving me as she stalks to the door.

The minute the door shuts behind her, I feel like I can finally breathe again. It's then that I realize Olivia is just sitting there looking stunned.

I turn to her and say, "Just so you know, she's wrong, I will never get tired of you. Lauren is a bitter, malicious woman who uses and abuses others. Don't believe a word she said."

Chapter Fourteen

LAUREN

You haven't heard the last of me, Vincent, Lauren thought as she stormed down the walk after having the door slammed in her face for the second time. *I'm going to get that money, one way or another. I don't have an option if I want to continue breathing. I'll do whatever it takes to ensure my survival.*

If I can't get the money out of Vincent or Pops, then I'll just have to use my son. Might as well make him good for something.

Chapter Fifteen

OLIVIA

"What's going on down here?" Junior asks from the bottom of the stairs.

"Nothing. Everything's okay. Go back to bed," Vincent says, pasting on a fake smile.

"Can you tuck me in again, Olivia?" Junior asks, clearly unsettled by the tension he can feel in the room.

"Of course, let's go."

"Olivia?" Junior innocently asks as we turn to go into his bedroom.

"Yes?"

"I wish you were my mom."

"I'd be honored, but I've never been a mom, Junior. I don't really know what a good one is like. My mom wasn't very nice, and we weren't close like you and your dad."

"But, you'd be a good mom! You could take care of Dad, too!"

"Thanks, that means a lot to me. I can't make any promises about becoming your mom, but in the meantime, I am your friend. For now, how about we be good friends?"

"I guess that's okay."

"Good because I'd like that. Now, it's time for bed," I say as he climbs under the covers.

"Sweet dreams," I say as I turn off the light and hurry out of the room before he can see how emotional. The truth is, I'd love to be his mom, and after meeting that woman, I know I'd be a better mom to him. I get my emotions under control quickly because I know I have to face Vincent.

By the time I get back to the living room, he's poured some wine for us both. When he sees me, he gets up, and brings my glass to me. I don't usually drink, but after tonight's events, I make an exception. I take a tentative sip, and it's not too bad. So, I take another bigger drink, and then start to feel calmer.

"It's a dessert Moscato. I thought maybe you'd like something sweet. Do you like it?"

"I do, thank you."

"Well, I guess we'd better talk," he says with resignation. "A lot of things have changed this evening."

Even though I know I shouldn't feel this way, my heart plummets because I'm afraid that reality has set in, and he's realized I'll never fit into his world. I'd already decided to leave before he answered the door, so I guess my plans haven't changed. My stupid expressive face must've shown exactly what I'm thinking.

"I think you're imagining something that's not going to happen," Vincent says with a knowing smile.

"We don't have to have the 'talk.' I know what you're going to say," I say jumping in before he can continue. "We can chalk this whole little experience to COVID messing with our brains."

"Wait, you think one glimpse of her, and I'm *ending* it?"

"Yes, and if I go now, I won't get hurt any more than I already am."

"Olivia, stop it. That's not it, just listen to me, please."

"Okay," I say, taking a sip of my wine to calm my nerves.

"I want you, and I know you want me, too. I care about you, and for the first time in years, I want a relationship."

"Vincent, let's be honest, you can do way better than me."

"Based on what?"

"You're you — unbelievably good looking, successful and mega rich. I'm me — plain, barely employable, and extremely poor. You probably find me interesting because we're so different, but that will get old quickly. When you realize I'm not going to magically turn into a debutante, you'll find someone who fits into your world better, and you'll leave me behind. You'll be fine, but I'll be yet another gullible girl in the world who slept with her boss and lost everything. I'll be exactly what *they* always accused me of being."

"Who?"

"My parents," I admit, taking a big gulp of wine.

"Listen to me, Olivia. Being a woman and enjoying a sexual relationship with a man does not make you a sinner. Enjoying life in general does not make you anything but human. You have nothing to be ashamed of, and I would never use you. That's not who I am. I don't love easily, but when I do, I mean it."

"What you say might be true, but t's difficult to ignore all the years of them pounding those ideas into my head. I've spent my whole life trying to live up to their expectations, and I was successful, until I met you. Being here with you makes me want to explore all those sinful desires."

A look of understanding crosses Vincent's face, then he asks, "So, until you met me, you'd never had alcohol, never kissed a man, never been tempted, or had a sexual dream?"

"No, never," I say. "Being with you like that today was the most pleasurable thing I've ever experienced, and definitely better than any dream. I'm scared if I stay here, I'll continue sliding down this slippery slope of lust and temptation."

"You're a passionate, beautiful young woman, not a sinner. The feelings you have for me are natural because you care about me."

"No—"

"Yes. I feel the same way about you. I always have."

"Vincent, I don't know if I can ever be what you want. I'm broken, and I may not be the person you think I am."

"You're not broken, and I'll help you get past what your parents said to you. We'll work on it together, I promise. However, I need to do some damage control. I need to go to Mexico to get my grandfather, and I have to figure out how to convince him to come back home. He's in a hospital in Mexico because he had a heart attack. Once I get that handled, we're going to work on our relationship because there is an us. For now, I just need you to know if you can get used to the idea of being my significant other?"

"How do I do that?"

"Let me cherish you, and trust that I care deeply and am not just using you. You'll also need to realize I'm aggressive when it comes to what I want, and not intimidated by it. I would never do anything to hurt you, however I will do everything to keep you here with us."

"I want to try, but it's going to be difficult to fight everything I've been taught my whole life."

"Give me a chance to prove how great we can be together. Can you do that?"

"I'm taking a huge leap of faith here, Vincent. Please don't betray me. I don't think I could recover from that."

"I would never do that to you, my sweet Olivia."

"Okay, then. I'll do my best. I think maybe we need to start by being open and honest with each other. So, I'd like you to start from the beginning. You can start with Lauren, then skip to the blackmail, then skip to how your grandfather came to be in the hospital." She says, and I agree. So, I tell her everything.

By the time I finish, I feel several different emotions, and at least two things have occurred to me. One, I loved talking to her, and number two, Olivia will be my wife one day, hopefully, soon.

"What are you going to do about her? She doesn't seem like the type who quits after one try."

"No, she's not. I'll deal with her, and if I have my way, she'll never get near any of us ever again. Lauren doesn't care about anything except Lauren, least of Junior. Her motivation behind her trying to insert herself in his life is one thing, and one thing only— money. Whatever is going on, she's desperate. However, that can wait, our priority is getting to Pops."

"You're really close, aren't you?"

"Yeah. My mom died giving birth to me, and my father never wanted anything to do with me because he blamed me for her death. He left right after her funeral, and no one has heard from him since. He could be dead for all we know. So, Pops raised me. My grandmother died from an aneurysm a long time ago, and since then no woman has been a part of our lives. It's just been us, the three Taylor men, since Junior was born."

"I'm sorry, Vincent."

"Don't be. Pops was the best parent ever."

"I'm glad you had him."

"Me too. I guess some people, like my dad and Lauren, just aren't cut out to be parents."

"What if I'm one of them?"

"You're not, I'd bet my life on it."

"You're clearly crazy. Okay, so what do you need me to do here while you go to Mexico?"

"Nothing, since you're coming with us."

"I'm going?"

"I want you with me, and I want you to meet Pops, and Patricia too."

"Are you sure? I don't mind staying behind."

"I mind, Olivia. I want you with me always, no matter where I am. Okay?"

This declaration has me teary-eyed. I'm not used to affection, especially this kind of affection, and it's a little overwhelming. I know him to be a man of his word, so I know he means it. This man has been nothing but good to me, he defends my honor, he includes me in his life, he treats me like I matter, and he doesn't judge me.

"Okay…I'd like that, I've never been to Mexico." I say with a shaking voice and hope in my heart.

***

The following morning, I wake up feeling like my whole life has shifted. At first, I feel a burst of happiness, but right on the heels of that feeling, is fear that I'm being too trusting. That I'm being naïve to believe that I deserve a life this or someone like him.

I go downstairs to start my day, and once again, Vincent joins me to prepare breakfast. This is usually my alone time, and him just turning up and shout-singing, "Good Morning!" he says, startling me, and causing me drop the dish I had in my hand."

"I'm sorry, I'm sorry, I didn't mean to scare you," he says with a chuckle as he helps me pick everything up. "I wanted to help you with breakfast, and give you this," he says, handing me an envelope.

"What's this?"

"It's your termination letter."

"What?"

"I meant what I said when I met you. We've blurred the lines already, but what's done is done. However, I'm not comfortable

continuing whatever this is as boss and employee. So, I decided to make some changes, effective immediately. I will hire someone else to assume your duties, and they will follow the same guidelines as Junior's teacher when she's here so that no one is exposed. From now on, anything you want to do here, you do because you want to, not because it's your job to do so. I want you to be comfortable in this growing relationship too, and I don't want you to feel as if I am taking advantage of you. I've also decided that it's not fair the position I've put you in, knowing you were probably depending on that salary. So, I've decided to provide you with the funds I promised when you accepted this position. I've slid the check under your door. It's blank, all you have to do is sign it to cash it should you ever need it. Consider it a severance package. This way, there will be no confusion on your part, or anyone else's as to how I feel about you, and who you are to me — my girlfriend."

"Vincent, it would've been nice if you'd discussed this next step with me last night so I wouldn't feel so blindsided. I've never been terminated."

"You're right, it was inconsiderate to do this without talking to you. Please forgive me?"

"Fine. You're forgiven."

"Thank you. Are you okay with this solution?"

"I guess so."

"You guess so?"

"Okay, yes. I'm more than okay with it," I say with a smile.

"Great. Now, we'll need to have a talk with Junior, so he knows what's going on. He should be down for breakfast any time now."

A few minutes later, Junior comes bounding into the room, "What's for breakfast? I'm starving!"

"Have a seat, big man," Vincent says, smiling at his son's exuberance. "Olivia and I want to talk to you about something while you eat." I put a plate filled with pancakes, scrambled eggs, sausage, and hash browns in front of him, then take a seat at the table.

"Mm, I can taste the syrup already," Junior says, as he grabs the syrup container, and drowns his pancakes. "You really need to have some!"

"Would you like the same thing he's having, Vincent?"

"Sure."

"So, as I was saying, we want to talk to you about a few changes." Vincent says as I place his plate in front of him, go get mine, and take a seat beside him. Junior slowly sits his fork down and looks up at us expectantly.

"Well, today we're all going to a clinic to take a COVID-19 test later this morning. Tomorrow morning, all of us, along with Patricia, will be going to visit Pops in Mexico. We're going to stay there for a while so we can take care of him."

"Did something happen to him?"

"Yes, he had a heart attack, but he's going to be fine. He just needs a little help for a while."

"Okay. Will the test hurt?"

"It will be a little uncomfortable, but I don't think it will hurt."

"Okay," he says, and goes back to devouring his breakfast.

"There's something else we wanted to talk to you about," Vincent says.

"Okay." He says as he continues to eat.

"I wanted to let you know that Olivia will no longer be working here, but —"

"You can't fire Olivia!" he stands and shouts indignantly.

"No! Junior, your dad didn't fire me. Well, he did, but—," Olivia starts to say when Vincent stops me.

"I did fire her, but I did it because she's agreed to be my girlfriend," I tell him anxiously.

"Wait, what?"

"I — we — wanted to ask if you had any problems with Olivia being my girlfriend."

"No! I think it's a great idea!" He says as he runs into my arms.

"So, this is cool with you?"

"Yes! Can she still stay here with us all the time, even after the lockdown is done?"

"Yes," Vincent says confidently at the same time I say no.

He turns to look at me and asks, "No?"

"Well, I just thought that maybe it's best if I—"

"No." Vincent says finally. I immediately look away to keep my emotions together and hide my discomfort when Vincent leans over to whisper in my ear. "We already discussed this. Trust me. Don't back out now. Trust me."

"Okay. Well, I guess the answer to your question is yes, Junior." I say turning back and addressing him directly.

"Great! Now that everyone's on the same page, hurry and finish your breakfast. We need to go take our tests."

After Junior goes upstairs, Vincent and I start cleaning up the breakfast dishes.

"How about you wash, and I dry?" he asks with a smile.

"You can dry. I have a feeling you're not accustomed to doing dishes." I say, smiling back at him.

"That's fine, too. I was just looking for a way to spend more time with you," he says, looking disappointed.

"I'd like that. Is this what having a boyfriend is like? I can get used to this." I say and he laughs.

"Part of it, yes. Essentially, a boyfriend is a partner. He's someone whose shoulder you cry on, someone you talk about your failures, success, hopes, dreams with, and vice versa. A relationship is when you do it all together, as a team." He says seriously.

"Yes, I'd love that."

"I just love being with you, no matter what we are doing." He says before dropping a kiss on my lips casually.

"Wow, this is the treatment I get after being fired?"

"In all seriousness, I want to spend as much time with you as I can. I want to get to know you — your likes, your dislikes … your body."

"Ok, uum, I don't necessarily know what to say to that. Besides, there's not really much to know, I'm pretty damn basic."

"You're anything but basic, baby," he says, grabbing me around the waist and pulling me close as I walk by.

"Vincent, Junior could walk in here at any moment."

"That's fine. You're my girlfriend now, and even he knows people who are boyfriend and girlfriend are prone to a little PDA.

"I don't want him to be uncomfortable."

"I think you're the one who's uncomfortable. Are you afraid of letting me touch you?"

"Honestly, maybe. I just need time to adjust, Vincent."

"Okay, then I'll give it to you." He says, stepping away from me when I grab his hand.

"Vincent, I hope you know that I do care, but you'll have to be patient with me."

"I'll be as patient as you need me to be, but you'll also have to step outside your comfort zone and meet me halfway."

"I'll try my best, I promise."

"That's all I can ask," he says as he turns me to face him, keeping his arms around me. "How about we seal it with a kiss?"

I look at him and he's so damn handsome. How can I resist him? I nod, and he kisses me tenderly until I just melt into him. The kiss deepens and goes from sweet to needy and hot in a flash, and I'm overwhelmed by feelings I've only dreamed of recently. I feel like I can't get close enough to him.

It's moments like this that it's so easy to hope that what he's telling me is true, and we do belong together. Deep down, I know it's what I want, but I don't know if I can quiet my inner demons enough to be what he needs.

"Dad, I'm ready to—" Junior says, bursting in and interrupting the moment.

I'm not just a little embarrassed, I'm mortified. "Oh, I'd better go get dressed," I say, practically running from the room.

"You know, Dad, that was kind of gross. Why do you want to swap spit with a girl?"

"You'll understand when you're older. By then, you won't think it's gross at all."

"Yeah, I don't think that's ever going to happen. I'm glad you like Olivia, though. I like her too."

"That's good to hear, big man. I'll go get dressed, and once Olivia's back down here, we will go."

Chapter Sixteen

VINCENT

A week later, we've been cleared of COVID, and we are leaving for Los Angeles, today. The days leading up to today have been exhausting to say the least. Junior has started "school" again, virtually, and he gets along with his new teacher famously.

We've finished Junior's classroom, and as it turns out, it was fun. What's even more surprising is the fact that it was as fun as it was *because* we did it together, like a family. I've been feeling guilty for that because Pops is my family, too.

I hate the thought of him being laid up in a hospital bed during this pandemic. I've had reports from the hospital, but it's not enough.

The only thing that's kept me from losing my shit these past days, is Olivia. She's been wonderful, and it almost feels like the three of us are a family already with one exception — she doesn't sleep in my bed. However, I am choosing to take an optimistic stance on the issue and push it to the back of my mind. If Pops can find love again after losing the love of his life, there's hope for me.

What I haven't been able to do is stop pondering why I didn't see it. Now that I've had time to think about it, he and Patricia make sense. She was his right hand; she anticipated his every need even before he does. Anywhere he was, she wasn't far behind. I should have seen it.

I keep thinking about the day he called me into his office and informed me of his retirement, and his decision to move out of the country. Looking back on it now, knowing what I know, I realize he did seem off that day, sad even. Before I could really ask questions and dig my heels in, our conversation was interrupted by a client wanting a detailed update on our progress on their site we were breaking ground on.

I'm pulled from my thoughts by Junior shouting, "Trish!!" as he runs up to her and hugs her. Olivia grabs my hand, and squeezes, giving me a reassuring smile.

"Thank you, I needed that," I mutter as I stand to greet my grandfather's girlfriend.

"Whatever you need, I'm here."

That was the perfect response. I give her a big smile as I watch as Junior and Patricia walk over to us, and I stand to greet her.

Regardless of the circumstances, I'm happy to see her. She been a maternal influence on Junior in a sense from the moment she came into Pop's life. Now, I realize how it must make her feel then and now to be so close to something you want and be told you can't have it. I hate that for her, for them.

"Hi, Patricia. Thank you for coming." I say, breaking the ice.

"Hi, Vincent. It's good to see you."

"You're looking well," I say, lying through my teeth. Patricia looks like hell, even though she tried to hide it with makeup.

She's dressed impeccably as always, but her eyes are sad, and she doesn't look like she's been sleeping well. I've never seen her with so much as with a hair out of place before, so I know she's coming undone over this whole thing.

I can only imagine how she's been beating herself up for not being there when Pops needed her. I pull her in for a long hug, and just like that, all the awkwardness fades into the background.

"Everyone needs to get to their seats and fasten their seatbelts, it's almost takeoff time." Janet, the flight attendant says. We all take our seats, buckle up, and not long after, we're in the air.

I grab Olivia's hand, and she smiles at me. It's amazing how natural it feels for her to be here with me. Thank God we were able to bypass an airport and TSA by not flying commercial and using our private runway and company jet as well as listing her as an employee for the company. There's no way her documentation would never have made it past TSA. Regardless, I'm happy she's here.

Currently, we're sitting on the tarmac as Patricia's bags are loaded.

So, for the first time since learning of Pop's incident, I relax, tilt lay my head back, close my eyes, and rest. Besides, this time in the air may be the only peace I'm going to have in a few days.

Sometime later, I wake with a start. I look down and see I'm still holding Olivia's hand, and she's resting. I look over to see Patricia and Junior watching a movie, and in that instant, I feel so glad Patricia decided to come.

The plane suddenly lurches, and the captain announces we've just hit some clear air turbulence. I look at Junior and Patricia, they seem to be fine, and then I look to my left. At the window, Olivia sits wide-awake, and clearly terrified.

"What's wrong, honey?"

"I don't like this," she says, her body tensing. "It's not safe."

The realization hits me like a ton of bricks. Shit! Of course, she's never been on a plane!

"Everything's fine, you don't have to worry. We just hit some turbulence. It's like a pothole in the sky — nothing to be afraid of," I say, squeezing her hand reassuringly. "How about a bottle of water and some Dramamine? It will help calm your nerves."

"Okay." She says shakily.

I hit the button to page Janet, and after the turbulence passes, she comes to see what I need, and shortly returns with a bottle of water and a pill.

She takes the pill, drinks some water, and swallows it quickly. I check my watch and note we're roughly an hour into the flight. "We're already a third of the way there. Ralph and Eric, my pilot and first officer, have years of experience, and they won't let anything happen to us. Try to relax.

"I don't know if I can."

"Okay, then let's talk. It will help pass the time and take your mind off it," I suggest.

"Okay. I can do that. What are we talking about?"

"What do you want to know?"

"Tell me about your first flight."

"Well, the company had been getting a lot of publicity, and the publicity brought on new investors. Pop's focus then was expansion from architect and engineering to commercial construction. Pops used the money from the investors to buy equipment and transportation. He bought compact track loaders, mini excavators, skid steers, dozers, excavators, wheel loaders, forestry machines, paving equipment, five company cars, and a MTOW Eclipse 500, and he was damn proud of it."

"I'd be too."

"Yeah. At the time, I was nine years old. I remember that day like it was yesterday. We were flying to Denver for a meeting with Richard Wentworth that day. He was an investor who ended up becoming best friends with Pops. Pops is a good man, but he doesn't have a good poker face. It was his first time flying in something so small, and he was just as terrified as me. I'll never forget the look on his face as we took off. He held my hand in a death grip until we were in the air," I say, smiling at the memory. "Even though I was terrified, I stared out the window the entire ride. The plane itself was one of only 260 produced that year. Now, you tell me something from your childhood."

"Oh, no. I don't have anything that … good to share with you."

"Anything you tell me about your life before me is interesting to me," I tell her as I kiss her on the cheek.

"So, what kind of plane are we in now?" She asks, deflecting, and I let her.

"This is the G550, it's made by General Dynamics' Gulfstream Aerospace out of Savannah, Georgia. It seats 19 and is equipped with state-of-the-art technology that makes flying in it extra safe. Trust me, this is way better than what I flew in then."

"If you say so. So, tell me something."

"Okay, shoot."

"Who was your housekeeper before me?"

"Uh, well I—"

"I already know. You created that position for me, didn't you?" I ask him.

"I was intrigued, yes, but I wanted to help you." I tell her as I kiss her hand and look into her eyes.

"Oh."

"Okay, it's my turn! Why did you accept my offer?"

"Well, I figured it was time to step out of my comfort zone and do something I really wanted. Accepting your offer is the exact opposite of what I'd usually do, so I did it."

"What do you mean?"

"I mean, I'm not a risk-taker. I don't have a life like most girls my age. I've always been a good girl."

"Who says you're not still a good girl?"

"My parents would say that. They'd be rolling in their graves if they knew what I've been up to," she says with a shaky smile.

"Well, *I* think you're a good girl. But you still haven't quite answered my question. What made you think I was worth stepping out of your comfort zone for?"

"Honestly, I don't know. I just knew you were a good guy, someone who kept his word, someone I could trust." she says solemnly.

"Well, I'm glad you did."

"Me, too. Now, it's my turn again. What are you going to do about your grandfather?"

"Well, get him healthy, preferably bring him back home with us. Once he's strong enough, I'm going to get some answers. I want to know why he felt he couldn't trust me."

"Vincent, that's not it at all," Patricia says, interrupting our conversation. "What your grandfather and I did was selfish, but we didn't mean to hurt you, and it certainly doesn't mean he doesn't trust you. Your grandfather is a proud and stubborn man, and he couldn't admit he loved another woman the way he loved your grandmother. In all the time we've been together, he couldn't admit that to me or himself, so it has nothing to do with how much he trusts you. Last week, I listened to his conversation with you, hoping he would finally tell you about us. It didn't happen, and I realized he was too comfortable with our lies.

"It was also clear to me that his pride means more to him than I do, so I left. I was tired of living a lie and I wanted to come home, so I gave him one more chance, and he said no. Now…I wish I'd never done that…If I'd been there, he wouldn't have been alone. I'm so sorry—"

"Stop it. This is *not* your fault." She says walking past us and taking a seat on the couch behind us. I immediately go to her and grab her hand and squeeze it.

"Patricia, this is not your fault, either. No one is to blame for causing this. I could blame Lauren, since she's the instigator here, but I'm sure the threat of his secrets being exposed caused his heart attack. That's on him. You made the right choice for you, and I know Pops would never hold that against you, even if it hurt him to see you go. I know deep down he understands why you left." I say and she hugs me, and I hug her back because I know she needs it, and I meant what I said. She trembles as she cries on my shoulders.

"I hope you know that Junior and I have always thought of you as family. Nothing would make me happier than you and Pops being together. I love you both, and you deserve happiness. I hope you two can work through this."

Patricia pulls away from me, and smiles sadly, and says, "I appreciate you for saying that. You don't know how much it means to me. I hope so, too."

"It'll be okay. We'll make sure of it." I say firmly. In this moment, I find myself praying for healing for everyone involved, and for what's to come next, because I get the feeling Lauren isn't done trying to cause trouble.

I feel Patricia start to relax in my arms, and after a few minutes she's pulled herself together. "Thank you, Vincent. I'm feeling better now, and I've come to a decision. I'm not letting him get away. I may have to drag him back home kicking and scream-ing, but we're moving back home and we're going to have a rela-tionship and life that's out in the open."

"Glad to hear it."

"Now, let's get to the good stuff. This must be the young lady I've been hearing about. From what I can tell, she's got you wrapped around her little finger."

"Well, I don't know about that part, but yes to the rest," I say, smiling.

"Well, she's beautiful and I can tell Junior loves her. He told me all about her and how happy he is that she's a part of your lives. It's about time, too. I'm happy you two found each other. Just remember, relationships take work. Treat every day like it could be your last one together, and you'll never lose what you have, I promise.

"Okay, I'll let you get back to your lady while I go to the lady's room and get my emotions in check before we land." She says before retreating to the back of the plane.

I get up and walk back to my seat next to Olivia, claiming her hand and giving her a reassuring look. "You're still nervous?"

"No, that pill worked."

"Good. Now you can enjoy the trip. If you feel brave, you might even look out the window."

"I'm fine right where I am. I don't want to think about it too much."

"Okay, ladies and gentlemen. We are approximately forty miles out. We'll be landing in the next fifteen minutes," the captain announces over the PA."

"Dad!" Junior yells, bounding over to us, "Before we left this morning, Ralph said if it was okay with you, I could sit up front with them in the extra seat! Can I?!!"

"That's fine," I say, laughing at his enthusiasm.

Turning, I see Patricia coming out of the lavatory I and ask her, "Are you familiar with the hospital and the area?"

"Yes. It's not too far from the house."

"Great. I want to get there as soon as possible. A car will be waiting for us when we land."

She smiles at me, and says, "You're just like him — taking charge and leaving nothing to chance. Do me a favor? Go easy on him."

"I'll try my best," I say, chuckling.

Twenty minutes later we pile into the waiting vehicle, and with Patricia's help, we make it to the hospital in no time. The driver stops at the emergency entrance and lets me out. I don my required mask and quickly walk inside. I want Pops out of here and back home as fast as possible.

Once inside, I go straight to the front desk and ask for Nurse Ramos. She comes out to greet me, gives me a quick update on Pops' condition, and informs me she's already got his discharge papers ready for me to sign.

In no time, they're wheeling Pops down the hall toward me. I quickly shoot Patricia a text to let her know we are coming out soon. I look up, my eyes meet his, and he quickly looks away. That's when I realize he's ashamed. I've never seen him admit to being wrong so easily before, and it's a little disconcerting. I might be mad at him, but at the end of the day he doesn't owe me an explanation for how he lives his life — he's a grown man.

"Pops, you didn't have to go this far just to get me to come down here and visit," I say, trying to lighten the mood.

He smiles weakly. "I'm sorry, son. I-I'm so sorry." he says, his voice breaking.

"We'll sort it out." I say as I lean down to give him a big bear hug, shaken by the thought that I could've lost him forever. "I've missed your old man. Now, let's get you out of here. There are some important people waiting to see you." I collect his things from the nurse, thank her, put his bag over my shoulder, and start wheeling Pops out of the hospital.

As we walk through the doors, I see everyone out of the car, at the entrance, waiting for us. The look of devastation in Pops' eyes when he sees Patricia is hard to take.

As Patricia comes towards us, they seem to communicate with their eyes, and I feel like I'm intruding on an intimate moment. I can see the deep sadness in her eyes mirrored in his, so I decide to give them some privacy, so I step away, and Patricia takes my place.

I start walking toward Olivia, and Junior runs up to Pops and gives him a big hug. I turn to watch and take a second to appreciate the scene before my eyes when they eventually wander to the woman who has turned my world upside down. She's looking back at me too, wearing a beautiful smile.

I can't believe how lucky I am. I don't care about her past or the ghosts of her parents, I just want to be with her and love her. My life feels complete in a way it never did before, and I don't want it to change.

"You're a sight for sore eyes," I say to Olivia as I close the gap between us.

"Really? You've only been gone twenty minutes, tops."

"Yes. It's been a difficult day but having you and Junior here has made all the difference."

"Well, I'm honored to be here."

"I'll let you in on a little secret."

"What?"

I smile and lean in closer so that only she can hear me. "I want you with me *everywhere* I go."

She looks up at me, and I can see the disbelief in her eyes. "Why?"

"Well, I—"

"So, this is Olivia!" Pops says as he rolls up in his wheelchair, sounding better than he did a few minutes ago in the hospital hallway. "I've heard nothing but great things about you, young lady. It's a pleasure to finally meet you, Olivia."

"I've heard great things about you, too, Mr. Taylor. It's nice to meet you as well."

"Pops, please. Not all bad, I hope. I know I'm not a favorite right now." he says as he looks at me and Patricia.

"Not at all, and from everything I heard about you, you are a favorite to me. I'm very glad to meet you." Olivia says, reassuring him, and making me want her even more.

***

The ride to Pops' home is mildly awkward, since Patricia isn't talking, and Pops won't look anyone in the eye. Those two have some serious talking to do if they want to save their relationship.

By the time all of us make it inside their house, I can tell we all needed a break. Before everyone can go off to their respective rooms, Patricia insists on giving a tour of the house and Junior says he's going to help her. Pops says he's tired and retreats to his room while the rest of us take the tour.

I'm not so sure this was a good idea though, because I see the look on Olivia's face as she steps into the foyer. I could read her thoughts like she'd said them out loud, and I know she feels out of place here. My house is certainly no closet, but it's not nearly as grand as this one.

To take away some of her unease, I wrap my arm around her shoulder and say, "You're part of this family now. You belong here, so get out of your head and enjoy the tour."

"Thank you," she says and smiles up at me, confirming my suspicion.

We chuckle at Patricia's Vanna White impression as she points out each feature as she describes it.

The house is amazing, and I'm a little envious of the home Pops built away from us. Maybe this can be a vacation home because Pops definitely needs to come back home with us. He certainly can't stay here alone; he's already proven that point. My thoughts are interrupted when Patricia announces the end of the tour.

After thanking her, Olivia and I walk Junior to his room., and he tells us he's going to play Mario Kart, so we leave him to his devices.

Based on the tour, there are two more rooms available upstairs, but I only see the need to utilize one. She may as well get accustomed to sleeping with me now. We come to a stop at the first door, and I turn to her. "Do you trust me?"

"Of course."

"Then, stay with me. Sleep in one room, with me."

"I don't know if I can do that."

"I understand it might feel like I'm rushing you, but I think things are moving at just the right speed. I'd never do anything to make you uncomfortable, so if you want, I can sleep in one of the guest rooms. Before you decide though, think of how nice it will be to wake up next to each other in the mornings. You agreed to try, remember? This is trying. Look at me. Nothing will take place that you are not ready or willing for. Do you understand?" I ask as I stare deeply into her eyes.

"Yes, I understand."

"Good. Now, let's go in."

We walk into the room and put our things away. Olivia sits on the bed and closes her eyes, and I choose that time to take a quick shower.

As I stand in the shower, I realize I've given her my heart, and the realization doesn't terrify me. *Who knew*? Before Olivia, I always viewed this type of relationship as something that made you too vulnerable. After all, I've seen two men absolutely destroyed by the loss of that kind of love, and only one of them chose to stay in my life.

Even though this is still so new, I already feel like I don't know what I'd do if I lose her. So, I'm going to take Patricia's advice, and work to make this relationship the best it can be.

Chapter Seventeen

OLIVIA

The following morning, I wake up with a smile on my face. It's unfamiliar, but I find that I prefer sleeping next to Vincent than sleeping alone. It's crazy! I've slept alone all my life and in one night, he's changed that.

I look at my watch to see that it's ten o'clock.

Shit! It's late! I look over my shoulder, and there he is. The damn man is as beautiful asleep as he is awake.

As I look at him, I think about the things I've learned from Pops and Patricia. I feel extremely touched by the praise Vincent and Junior have apparently been laying at my feet based on what Patricia and Pops have said. It forces me to reconsider; maybe I really do mean as much to Vincent as he claims. Vincent's grandfather clearly means the world to him, so if I was a brought up to him, then more than likely, he doesn't have casual intentions which only scares me more.

Once again, I get the feeling I've been dropped into someone else's life. I swear, my life has become just like my favorite billionaire erotica book, *Fifty Shades*. In some ways, that's exciting and in others, it's terrifying!

I can't help but to imagine Vincent in the role of Christian Grey and me as the innocent, sexy Anastasia Steele when I'm reading the series. In my fantasies and, I want to be the girl he's doing all these unspeakable things to, even though it's uncharted territory for me.

I've been trying to learn what I can about sex through research in the form of erotic books, online porn, and the internet. Every time that I do, I feel overwhelmed and extremely *"vanilla"* as they call it.

Based on all my research, I think there must be something thrilling and life-changing about the act itself. Vincent certainly makes me feel the things I read about, desire and lust. I love the way he looks at me, touches me, and kisses me. At night I find myself touching myself and imagining it's his hands. Still, the fact remains that I'm not sure I'm prepared to be his girlfriend and all that entails.

Every time I think of Vincent, I'm assaulted butterflies in my stomach. Sometimes he looks at me like I'm one of the most cherished things in his life and I forget to breath. But can I be what he needs? Can I belong here? How does someone like me get used to living like this after living dirt poor? Am I capable of living in this wealthy, privileged world?

Ugh! I need to get out of my head and just focus on the present and let it all play out.

I don't know why, but at the back of my mind is the thought that Lauren wouldn't feel out of place here, it would fit her like a glove. I hate the way I keep mentally revisiting in my mind how she looked at me; like a fly to be swatted away or dirt on the bottom of her Christian Louboutin's.

Maybe it will work out. It is a great feeling to be with someone so competent, and experienced. Maybe I can just trust him to lead us where we need to go.

***

"You're awake." Vincent says as he rolls over and pulls me closer to him.

"I am."

"What are you thinking about?"

"You."

"What about me?" He pushes, and I smile at his playfulness.

"Things."

"Okay, okay, I'll leave it alone. It's still early, I wonder who else is up."

"I haven't heard anyone moving around."

"Good, I need a shower." He says, jumping up and out of bed as I lay down, watching him. "Want to join me?"

I try to act cool, though I am completely out of my element, and about to lose my shit. "I'm scared to. I've never seen a man naked before."

"And you won't, unless it's me." He says.

After a moment's hesitation, I say "Yes. I want to join you."

"Only if, you're sure."

"I'm sure, but you get in first and I'll come in behind you."

"Okay, I'll be waiting," he says gently before disappearing into the bathroom that we share.

He leaves the door slightly ajar, and I hear the shower start a few seconds later. I imagine him taking off his shirt, revealing those six-pack abs and broad shoulders I love to look at. Then undoes the button on his pants, unzips, and slowly takes them off. With a start, I realize I'm turned on by this little fantasy. Will today be the day I get over my fear and finally act on these things I've been imagining?

I walk over and peek into the bathroom through the crack in the door. There's steam billowing out of the shower, and I can see Vincent's silhouette. He' so fit — I can see muscle definition even from here. *How can this Greek statue come to life really be interested in me?* I wonder for the millionth time. I'm sure he's been with lots of women, so I don't know how I can ever measure up.

How will I ever be able to compete with all the other rich, sexually experienced women out there lusting after him? Can I really take a chance that he's telling the truth about everything and admit how I truly feel about him?

I decide to be brave and step outside my comfort zone for once. I could get hurt, but I could also finally be happy and loved for who I am.

My heart rate picks up, and I feel like I'm about to have a panic attack. I'm not backing down though. I'm going to take the plunge. He's worth it.

The shower keeps running and suddenly, Vincent's standing there, water dripping from his hair, naked as the day he was born, and he was beautiful.

He smiles his sexy smile and scorches me with his intense stare. "See something you like, Olivia?"

"Um…"

"Are you enjoying your little peep show?" he asks, chuckling.

"Uh, yeah," I say, blushing furiously. "Sorry."

"Don't be. I'm certainly not. In fact, I liked it." The way he's looking at me, like the way a lion looks at prey, is a bit terrifying.

"Vincent, you know we're going to have to take things slow, right?"

"Trust me, I know. I'm doing everything I can to slow myself down. It's all I can do to keep my hands off you."

"Maybe I don't want you to keep your hands off me, Vincent. I just don't know exactly what to do about it."

"You'll figure it out, but there are some things I'd like to show you. I promise we'll go slow. You can trust me, Olivia. I'd never do anything to intentionally hurt you."

"I do trust you, but some of my fear has nothing to do with you. It's my parents' voices, their beliefs and thoughts in my head telling me I'm going to hell for giving into sins of the flesh."

"You are *not* going to hell. From what I can tell, God is very forgiving, so hell is not an option for you. You have a good heart and nothing you do in this lifetime is going to send you anywhere but Heaven. Your parents are dead and gone, don't let them control you anymore. You're the only one who controls your life now."

"You're right. I do give them too much power. I want to … continue what we were doing in the laundry room before the door rang, but you're going to have to walk me through it."

"Okay, just follow my lead, enjoy, and just feel. If we get to a point where you're too uncomfortable, all you need to do is tell me to stop. You're the boss here. Okay?"

"Okay."

"I think you're wearing too many clothes for a shower," he says, looking down at me. "Want me to help you out of them?"

"No, I can do it," I say, feeling more confident than I did a few seconds ago.

I lift my blouse over my head, and he begins to trail kisses down my neck to the edge of my bra. Then, he unbuttons my jeans, pulls the zipper down and slides them and my panties to the floor. "Step on out of those, baby."

I do as he asks and stand in front of him in only my bra, and I feel two things — terrified and excitement.

Before another moment passes, Vincent quickly unsnaps my bra, and slowly pulls me into the shower with him. Vincent pulls me under the water with him, grabs my chin and pulls me into a kiss that leave me aching and unstable on my feet.

In between my legs, I feel wetness, and an aching like no other, and I have no idea what to do to satisfy it, but he does. I'm so lost in the kiss that when he takes my hand in his and wraps it around his penis, I don't hesitate to follow his movements.

In my hands, he feels like nothing I've ever touched before — hard and soft all at once. I can feel it throbbing and growing harder from my touch somehow. I never imagined something like this would make me feel so powerful, but that's exactly what it's doing.

Vincent grips my hand and guides it so I'm holding tighter and stroking him up and down. He groans, and I stop immediately. "Did I do something wrong?"

"No, baby. Please don't stop," he says, then claims my mouth.

I continue to stroke him, and when his hen the kiss ends, I'm left stunned and breathless, and I've completely forgotten what I was doing until his manhood jerks in my hands, and I jump. "Don't worry. He's just excited. You're so beautiful, my Olivia." He says, before blazing a hot trail over my skin with his hands, leaving goosebumps in his wake.

I've never felt anything like this before. It's like I'm on fire and I'm about to explode, just from his touch. He moves around to stand behind me and kisses my neck as he massages my breasts from behind, making me moan. Gasping, I move to cover my mouth when he stops me. "Don't do that. I want to hear you; I want to hear it all."

"But—"

"No buts, I want all of you," he says as turns me and kneels in front of me, looking in my eyes the whole time.

As I look down at him, he bends to slide his tongue along the edge of my private place, inhaling deeply. The pleasure it brings, the surrealness of him in between my legs, the horror, all of it, sends me on an out of body experience as I long for something I can't name.

"Mm, you taste as delicious, but I want more." he says as he proceeds to place both my hands on his shoulders, and lifts one of my legs and hooks it over his shoulder giving him more access to me. "Just relax and enjoy."

My hips buck involuntarily, and I open my leg wider, giving him more access. I want more of that feeling. When he penetrates me with his tongue, as his fingers thrust in and out of me, I lose control. Before I know it, my hands are on either side of his head, holding him in place as his tongue and fingers reap havoc on my nerves.

His left-hand travels up to circle my nipple, and a second later, he starts tongue-fucking me, his tongue taking place of his fingers, in and out. His relentless licking, swiping, and sucking builds a combination of pressure until it's too much, and I exploded from the pleasure. He doesn't stop his efforts until my body spasms again and I push his head away.

"Vincent, I can't. I can't take anymore."

"Okay, but next time, don't push me away when you cum. I want to taste your orgasm on my tongue." He says as he stands back up and kisses me. From his tongue, I taste me, and surprisingly, it tasted good.

He smiles down at me and asks, "What do you think? Did you enjoy that?"

I look up at him and nod my head overcome and overwhelmed to speak.

"I'm not done with you yet. I think there are a few more climaxes you can reach before we're done for the evening."

Any thoughts I had vanish as he starts working his magical tongue and fingers again. Even though I didn't think I could stand anymore, my body disagrees, and that delicious pressure is already there again. When the pleasure comes crashing down again, the only thing I can do is submit.

Chapter Eighteen

VINCENT

"I think part one of your introduction from good girl to good woman went well." I say jokingly as I kiss her on the forehead.

"Yes, I suppose it did."

"Suppose? Do I need to demonstrate again?" I say as I start to tickle her. Her laughter is literally medicine to my soul. This is true happiness.

"Vincent, we need to go downstairs, and see who is up. Maybe I can make or help with breakfast."

"Yeah, your right. Yesterday was pretty raw and exhausting for everyone, I think. I've never seen Pops look so fragile, and it damn near broke me. He's the strongest man I've ever known, and I've never seen him be anything but confident in everything he does."

"I think he'll be fine. He and Patricia will get things straight, and I think you and he need to have a discussion too. I'm sure he'll be strong enough to have a talk with you soon. It was just a mild heart attack, right?" She asks, shocking me with her words. I had no idea she could be so perceptive.

"Yes, it was mild, but what if it wasn't? What if he died with all of these lies between us?"

"He didn't, that's all that matters."

"I know. It was just a shock to the core to realize, to see actually proof that he's not immortal, and he won't always be around. Seeing how badly he's fucked up with the love of his life has only opened my eyes more."

"How so?"

"Well, I realize I've been lying to myself about why I've been keeping my distance from any commitments all these years. After Lauren, I was scared to open my heart and my life to anyone other than Junior and Pops, until I met you. I've been trying to be patient because I know my usual aggression will only scare you away. However, seeing the beauty of second chances, I've decided to seize the day and put everything into what makes me happy — and you and Junior are what makes me happy."

"How can you be so sure I'll continue to make you happy after all of this has passed?"

"Because I've been in love with you for months."

"*What?*"

"Yes, and eventually you will realize that you love me too, but until you do, I'll just do my best to convince you."

"I do feel something Vincent, but I'm not sure it's love, because I don't have anything to compare it to."

"I know, don't worry. We'll navigate those waters together."

"I'd like that."

"Me too." He says as he pulls me in for a tender kiss to the forehead.

"Can I ask you something that's a little off topic?" She asks.

"Of course, shoot."

"What are you going to do about Pops?"

"Well, maybe I won't have to do anything. If he and Patricia put their hurt feelings aside and talk to each other, they can work through this, and she might stay. However, if she doesn't, it's not an option for him to be so far away from me, alone. I'd still love for them to be back in Florida, or at least closer. I think the whole point of having this place was so he could live his life without any questions or judgement. That's no longer an issue, or it shouldn't be."

"I get it. Maybe things will change once he realizes that you accept him and his choices. I saw what you did. In your own way, you gave them you're blessing without saying the words. Eventually, it will make a difference to him."

"I hope so. He needs a swift kick in the ass. Enough about them, I want to talk about you. I want to ask you a question." I say, turning her to face me.

"What about me?"

"Why do you allow people, money, and things to intimidate you? Why is your reflex to run away?"

"I don't know. It may have something to do with my upbringing, but really, I struggle with how to act around people like you and Pops."

"Like yourself. We're human like everyone else, and you have first-hand experience knowledge of that. The money, the jets, the cars, and houses don't really mean anything in the grand scheme of things. We want to love and be loved like everyone else."

"I know your people…now."

"Good."

"Now, can I ask you something?"

"Yep."

"Okay, have you seriously considered what the tabloids and everyone else will say about us? Do you understand the story they will spin about the poor maid, and the rich billionaire boss? How will they say our relationship came to be? The public will never see me as your equal, and they will not accept me. They'll look at me just like Lauren did."

"Listen, I can't change who I am any more than you can change who you are, but I do want to apologize for not realizing how my celebrity would affect you. I'm accustomed to the media, but you are not, and I should have been mindful of that. I do know that regardless of anything being said about us, separately or together, we'll weather together, and I'll protect you as much as I can. Just trust in me and trust that everything will fall into place.

"Vincent, you can't protect me from everything."

"We'll see about that." I say, as I pull her in for a kiss.

"No, no, none of that. We should probably go check on Junior and everyone else. We don't want to be bad houseguests."

"You're right. I'll let you take your shower first."

Chapter Nineteen

VINCENT

I lay there smiling as I watch the extraordinary woman beside me jump out of bed and run into the bathroom. This part is new for me too. Lauren and I never got to this part, living, and sleeping together, which is probably for the good.

I've got a serious case of blue balls, but this morning was definitely worth it. What we did today was a huge step for her. I'm just surprised and in awe of what she is willing to try for me despite the thoughts running around in her head telling her everything we have, everything that we are doing is bad.

The more Olivia tells me about her parents, and what they said to her, the more suspicious I become. There's more to their story than what Olivia knows. They seem like they were cruel and calculating people who carefully orchestrated her life so they could control exactly what she did, who she knew, and spoke to.

When she told me about her mother saying she had "whore's blood" running through her veins, it made me even more curious. Mothers just don't say that kind of thing to their daughters. Something's not right, and I'm going to find out what it is. The problem is, it's past time I tell her about my suspicions. I can't preach honesty and love when I'm keeping a secret like this from her concerning her.

My phone begins vibrating on the dresser, pulling me out of my thoughts. I don't feel like moving, but it may be Lawrence and with Lauren on the loose, I need to take it. I get to my phone right before it goes to voicemail. "Hello?" I say.

"Hola, Señor Taylor. Como estas?"

"Hola, Mr. Santorini. I'm doing well. How are you and Maria?"

"We are good, staying safe. This pandemic is not good for business."

"No, not at all. Everyone at Taylor has been working from home since the lockdown started."

"I'm sorry to hear that."

"Me, too. So, what's on your mind?"

"Well, Maria and I wanted to discuss something with you. It's something new we want to try."

"We agreed that you and Maria would make all the business decisions. I'm just a silent partner, and I will support whatever you decide to do. I trust your judgement completely. You don't need my permission, Pedro."

"I know, but it's your investment and business, too." He says, and I smile at that.

"My money may have started it, but you two finished it. You don't owe me anything, my friend."

"Okay, but I still want to run our idea by you. You are the businessman; we want your honest review of the business plan we are putting together going forward."

"Okay, let's hear it."

"All of the cafes have closed. There's no need for a coffee before work without a job to go to. We want to open the restaurant side up. We don't have everything dining wise yet, but since no one will be dining in, that's okay. We have all the licenses and certifications for the health department. All the restaurants nearby have converted to contactless deliveries, and we want to open up the kitchen and offer the same thing. We looked at the budget and we think it could work. That way we can stay open during lockdown and make money through this thing. I can hire a few delivery drivers, and some cooks. Maria and I are working on putting a menu together. What do you think?"

"It sounds like a smart move to me, so do what you think is best. Email me the details. I'll run the numbers, and let you know if I have any suggestions. Sound good?"

"Yes, Señor Taylor. I'll have it to you by Monday morning."

"Great. I'll look at it first thing so you can get it going quickly. Talk to you soon, and please give Maria my best."

"I will. Goodbye, Señor Taylor."

I hang up and smile. They just can't seem to understand that I trust their business instincts.

"Santorini's, isn't that the name of the shop where we met?" Olivia asks as she comes back into the room, wet and wrapped in a towel.

"Yes, it is."

"So, you weren't just a fan of the coffee there?" She asks, referring to the explanation I gave her for my presence the day we met. I can't help but to smile at that.

"Yes, well maybe it's a bit more than that."

"Like being an owner?"

"Yes, exactly."

"Why didn't you tell me you owned it?"

"I don't know. I didn't really think about it."

"Hmm, okay. So, what's next?" She asks, pulling back the towel and giving me a spectacular view as she sits on the bed. *Damn! We need to get out of here, now!*

"Let's get dressed and figure that out."

***

Twenty minutes later, finally showered and dressed; we go to check on Junior. He's not in his room, and Patricia and Pops are MIA, too. So, we head downstairs to find them. As we move from room to room, I notice something odd — everywhere I look there are drawings and paintings of beautiful buildings signed "LR".

Are these all by the infamous architect Louis Reed? Why does Pops have so many paintings by this guy?

When we get to the living room, I notice the sliding glass doors that lead to the patio are slightly open. We step out onto the patio and are hit by the delicious smell of food, music, and laughter to our left.

We follow the sounds and see Junior splashing around in the hot tub, with Pops and Patricia keeping watch over him. We head in their direction,

"Hey, everybody!" I shout as we come approach them and sit down.

"Hey! How was your rest, sleepyheads?" Pops asks.

"We didn't want to wake you, we figured you needed the rest after all the excitement of this week." Patricia adds, "When we heard Junior up and about, we thought we'd give him something to do to keep him busy so you could rest longer. I made us some things to snack on, feel free to have some," she says, indicating all the enticing looking food and drinks spread out on the table.

"We appreciate it, thank you Patricia," I say as Olivia gets up and grabs a plate for us both and starts filling it with a variety of food. As she returns with the plates and settles back in next to me, I look over to Pops and address him.

"I noticed you have quite the Louis Reed collection, Pops. Did you commission all of them for this house?"

"Maybe we should give you two some privacy," Patricia says, as she starts to get up.

"No, you don't have to leave. It's time," Pop says.

She sits back down, and Pops starts talking, "Son, I've hidden enough about my life from you, and it's time I stop keeping secrets. While I was recovering, I realized I just can't continue the way I have because my heart can't take it. So, to answer your question, no, I didn't *commission* those Louis Reed paintings, I *am* Louis Reed."

"I don't understand." I say, setting down the fork full of food I was about to eat.

"In school, I discovered my talent for architecture, however it was the business side of things that I had a passion for. When I started the company, I didn't have a partner and I had very little money. I hadn't found enough investors to hire even one good architect, so I became one. In doing so, I found my voice as the artist in me began to develop. I could look at any property, space, or abandoned building, and see it's hidden potential. After losing a few jobs to bigger firms, I was desperate to get the company up and running. I had a wife and a baby on the way, so I needed a steady income."

"I had to improvise to get the attention of the bigger clients and be put myself in the league with the bigger firms. I did that by claiming I had a private, but amazing, corporate architect, Louis Reed, who could deliver amazing results on any project. Everything I showed them — the portfolios and all the designs — were really mine. I wasn't licensed and I couldn't let it get out that I lied about the firm's 'star architect' to land big accounts. So, Louis Reed has remained a secret all these years."

"Eventually, I was licensed, but by that time everyone wanted Louis for their projects. I couldn't just make him disappear, so for ten years, Louis continued to design for our company, helping to build its reputation. When we went public, I was finally able to retire him permanently. When we moved, I began to draw and create for me, for fun, and I decorate my walls with the results. I'm sorry I lied to you for so long, son."

By now, I'm livid and holding onto my control by a thread. "More lies and secrets? I look at you and I see the face of the man who raised me, but otherwise, you're a perfect stranger to me. The man I thought I knew would never hide something like this. I'm the fucking CEO of your empire, and now I find out it was built on lies." I say, completely dumbfounded.

Was Lauren right? What else don't I know?

I take a deep breath and try to calm down. "Don't get me wrong, I'm glad you feel so free here, but I hate the fact that you felt so caged with us that you thought it was necessary to move so far away to be yourself!"

"It's not that son, it's—"

"Son? Right about now, I'm not sure I want that title! It implies a certain trust and respect that you clearly never had for me. I need some fresh air," I say as I make a quick exit.

"Vincent, wait!" Olivia calls from behind me.

"I need to get out of here and clear my head. You can stay if you want," I say without turning around.

"Vincent, at least hear him out," Olivia pleads.

"I need some time to wrap my head around the fact that the person who raised me isn't the man I thought he was. Look at where we are, Olivia. He came here because he has too much pride to own up to his lies. Who knows how long I would've been in the dark if Lauren hadn't tried to blackmail him!" I say before walking off.

I go through the kitchen, see car keys hanging from a peg on the wall, I grab them, and head to the garage. When I open the door to see several cars, so I hit the fob and the Audi at the very back chirps back at me. I walk over to it and hop in, hit the garage door remote, and roar off down the drive before the door is even fully open.

I drive aimlessly for a while, before pulling into an empty parking lot. I need to gather my thoughts, so I park and sit there, trying to deal with my hurt feelings.

I can't believe Pops has kept so much from me. I've always told him everything about my life, even when it didn't involve him directly. But this *did* involve me. He ran off to hide without telling me why, leaving me to run a company that was built on his lies. I understand what he did for the business, hell I'm glad he had the balls and the talent to back it up. It's impressive as hell by what he was able to achieve. But to keep it from me when he's groomed me to run his business since I was a kid? I just don't get it. This is making me doubt everything I thought I knew about him, and how he feels about me.

I was so preoccupied with my thoughts that I didn't realize a car had pulled up beside me. I can't see inside because the windows are tinted, so I'm surprised when the passenger door opens, and Pops gets out of the car. I sigh, then laugh at the irony of how well he knows me. He comes over and knocks on the window. After I roll it down, he asks, "Mind if I join you?"

"Do you really care if I mind?"

"Of course, I do."

"Whatever. Get in," I say, unlocking the passenger door. I watch as he signals to the driver, probably Patricia, and it makes a U-turn, heading back toward the house. Pops watches the car until it is out of sight, then opens the door and slowly gets in.

"How'd you find me?"

"I have a tracker on the car, and apparently it works really well. Besides, it wasn't rocket science trying to find a guy driving a cherry red Audi Q7."

"Guess we can add detective and comedian to your list of hidden talents."

"I understand you're angry and hurt, and I am sorry for it. I wish I could take it back, but I can't. What's done is done," he says, with a resigned sigh.

"I feel … blindsided Pops. I thought we were close. I thought I knew everything there was to know about you."

"We *are* close, don't doubt that."

"So, why all the secrets?"

"It had nothing to do with you. It was all about me. I didn't mean to hurt you."

"Right, I suspect that's because you never expected to have to come clean. I understand about the designs and why you did that? Why did you never tell me? What about Patricia? Did you really think I'd condemn you for finding love again? How did things get so twisted around that you felt it was best to come here to hide your relationship and your work from me? I just don't understand.

"Well for starters, I felt like I was betraying my wedding vows when I fell in love with Patricia. Loving another woman just didn't seem right to me. Your grandmother was the love of my life, and I thought I'd only have one of those."

"Don't you think Gram would want you to be happy? I'm positive she wouldn't want you to be alone for the rest of your life."

"Maybe, but there's really no way I can know that for sure."

"I think you know."

"Maybe I kind of do, I just … I never wanted to fall in love again because I never wanted to have to feel the kind of loss I felt when I lost your grandmother. I didn't think I could survive that kind of pain a second time, so I decided I'd never take that path again. When Patricia came into my life, I just couldn't give her up. I'm a coward for hiding her away, and I let her down. I don't deserve her, and I can't know if I can give her what she wants most."

"I think you can, Pops. It's your choice. I understand a little more now, but if you want to move forward, you're going to have to start being honest with everyone — including yourself."

"I know, son."

"Yeah, you do. You'd better come to the right answer too, or you're going to have to deal with Junior and me being mad at you," I say, and smile knowingly at him. "I'm so glad you're okay, Pops. I thought I was going to lose you. You need to get your life and your health together because I can't live in a world without you, Pops."

"I know and I will, believe me," he says emotionally as he pulls me into his arms for a hug. We pull away from one another, and smile. "It's good to see you so happy. Our plan obviously worked out for you, huh?" He asks with a smile.

"Oh, man, we have a lot to catch up on."

"I've got all the time in the world. Want to go for a beer? I know a place that's probably open, but I'll warn you, it's not the nicest."

"You know I don't care about that. C'mon, let's go." I say.

Ten minutes later, we ended up in a booth inside a hole-in-the-wall bar, which was all but deserted. After the waitress brings our drinks, we settle in, and we talk like nothing ever happened, and no time has been lost.

"So, that viper Lauren really thought she was going to get somewhere with you by just showing up on your doorstep and pretending she wanted to see Junior?" Pops asks, before taking another swig of his beer.

"Yeah, but I didn't have time to really deal with her because I got the call from the hospital telling me what happened within a few minutes of shutting the door in her face."

"Hmm. Must've been fate."

"Maybe. Now that I know you're okay, I need to figure out what to do about her. I don't think she's giving up that easily. She's desperate for some reason and desperation is dangerous for a woman like her."

"You could involve the police."

"I could, and most likely will, but I think it's going to take more than a restraining order to stop her. I want her out of our lives forever, I just need to figure out how to make that happen."

"Should I be worried? You're not thinking of hiring a hitman, are you?"

"No, of course not. No matter how much I wish she'd just go away, I'd never do something like that."

"Just making sure, though I would understand the temptation." He says, laughing.

"Trust me, if I knew how I could live with that, I'd do it in a heartbeat. However, I can't, so I've got Lawrence digging into her finances to find out what she's been doing the last few years. I should hear something from him soon."

"Let me know what you find out."

"You'll be the first one I call."

"So, what else is going on?"

"How do you know there's more?"

"Hah! It's written all over your face."

"I need some advice about how to tell Olivia about my discreet investigation into her past. I haven't told you everything, but there have been some red flags surrounding her identity."

I go on to tell him everything, including the circumstances of our meeting, her interview with the company, what was discovered by the company's fraudulent specialists, and the fact that she seems unaware of it all. "I can't put my finger on it, but the more I hear about her childhood, the way her parents treated her, the more I think there's something more going on here. It's just a feeling at this point, but I want to be sure there's nothing more to it than them being extremely bad parents."

"From the sound of it, you don't need my advice, son — you want my approval, but you don't need it. This is the woman you have chosen, and you're trying to protect her. You unturn whatever stone needs to be unturned to do so. My only advice is don't treat this like you would a business decision— logically and with no regard for feelings. This is her life, and she may not take kindly to you digging around in it without her knowledge. Solving the mystery won't mean anything if you lose her in the process. If you're right, she probably needs to know."

"Thanks for your input. I will be sure to take that into consideration."

"I'm just happy you'd still want my opinion on anything."

"Pops, just because you've been an ass, it doesn't change the fact that I value your insight. I'm sorry I've been so hard on you. It's not my place to question or judge any of your actions."

"I deserved it. I'm sorry I hurt you, son."

"It's okay, I understand."

"Good. Now, let's get back to the house before you piss your girl off more."

"What do you mean?"

"Hate to break it to you, but you're in the doghouse, son."

I instantly think about the way I left and feel guilty for leaving Olivia alone in an environment and with people that are unfamiliar to her. "Yeah, I guess I deserve it if she is. Let's get going."

"Cherish it, even in moments like this." He says, and I look over at him in understanding.

"C'mon Pops, you mean you're going to let Patricia come all this way and then just let her leave again? She's a mess, and she's barely holding it together. I think you still have a chance with her, but you need to confront your fears. This could have been your second chance, Pops. She loves you, but the way you've been hiding your relationship doesn't work for her anymore. You're going to have to do some major groveling and then ask that woman to marry you. It's time to pull out all the stops. We want you guys to be together and move back to Florida. We miss having you around."

"Whoa! One thing at a time, son. Marriage, I need to wrap my head around, but as for the rest, I have no real objections. I miss being near you all too."

"You know, you're very wise. I wonder where you got it from."

"Well, I had a wise teacher," I say as he laughs, pulls me in for a hug, and slaps me on the back. "Now, let's get the hell out of here, and win our women back."

Chapter Twenty

OLIVIA

By the time Vincent makes it back to the house, I, along with everyone else had retired to their bedrooms for the evening. When he opens the door to the bedroom, the lights are off, and it takes a minute for my eyes to adjust. I can see the shape of him approaching the bed, but I turn away. I hear rustling, which I can only assume is him shedding his clothes before climbing in bed next to me.

"Are you awake?"

"I'm not talking to you," I say to him, standing my ground even as I rejoice in his closeness.

"Look, I'm sorry about earlier. I just needed to get away before I said something I'd regret."

"I get that, but I don't appreciate you leaving without telling me where you were going, or when you'd be back. You acted like a jerk, and you just ran off. I'm in a foreign place in someone else's house, Vincent."

"I am truly sorry. I wasn't thinking. I just had to put some distance between me and Pops so I could clear my head."

"Did he find you?"

"Yeah. We had some beers and talked."

"Well, I guess that's good. Did you get things straightened out?"

"We did, but I don't think it's me he needs to fix things with the most, it's Patricia."

"I think so, too. I hope they work it out. I like her, and she's been nice to me. We sat, talked, and drank wine as we waited for you two to get back."

"Good, I'm glad you were able to get to know her better. See? Some good came out of my leaving when I did. Am I off your bad side?"

"For now," she says, and laughs.

"Are you laughing at me, Miss Hunt?" He asks, wrapping his arms around me.

"What if I am?"

"Now, you're sassing me too! That's it! I guess I've got to teach you a lesson," he says, taking my mouth in a deep kiss meant to lead to more. I love the way he moans and touches my breasts. *I think maybe he's unleashed a wildcat.*

"Vincent?"

"Yes?"

"I want you to make love to me right now," I say, and he goes completely still against me.

"You can't imagine how much I want you, Olivia, but I want our first time to be special — not a spur-of-the-moment thing. I want to cherish you, honor you, and make love to you for the rest of my days — just not yet." He says and I remain silent for a second, processing his rejection.

"Sweetie, I'm not saying I don't want to be with you," I say quickly, trying to smooth things over. "It's just—"

"Let's just get some rest," I say, turning away from him, and effectively ending the conversation.

Sleep was elusive, but eventually, my mind calmed enough to allow me some rest. However, the first thing I remember is the stinging rejection Vincent delivered last night.

I can't believe I finally get up the courage to offer myself to him and he refuses. I don't know why it hurts so much, I knew eventually he'd come to his senses and realize we don't fit together. I guess the disappointment comes from the fact that I hoped in the first place.

An apparent glutton for punishment, I replay his words, "I want to cherish you, honor you, and make love to you for the rest of my life."

Wait, what?

Did he hint that he wouldn't make love to me until we're married? I'm just getting used to being his girlfriend, and now he expects marriage. Do I even want that?

These mixed signals are making me dizzy. Maybe I should've let him explain last night because now things are going to be awkward between us.

"You're awake," Vincent says, his breath puffing into my hair as he tightens his arms around me.

"Yes, I'm awake," I say, rolling out of his embrace and getting out of bed. "I'm going to go shower and then see if I can help with breakfast."

"Come on, don't run from me. Can we talk about last night? Please?"

"Vincent, I need some time to think and process. My feelings are hurt, and I need to get them under control. I don't want to say something hurtful that I can't take back."

"The only way you can hurt me is by walking out on me. Is that what you're doing?"

"No. I just—"

"Then, just tell me what's going through your head."

"Okay," I say, sitting back down on the edge of the bed.

"What do you think happened?"

"Well, first you introduce me to sex, you touch me and lick me and make me want things I've never wanted before. Last night, I offered myself to you, you rejected me, and in the same breath tell me you want to spend the rest of your days with me. What does that mean? Everything with you is too much, too fast, and I'm overwhelmed."

"I know, I'm sorry. I got ahead of myself, and I didn't mean to overwhelm you. I apologize."

"Vincent, we've been a couple for a hot minute — literally, weeks, and I don't even know if I'm doing that right — and you're already casually talking about bigger commitments. Again, it's too much, and too fast."

"Well, you're a great girlfriend, you don't have to worry about that. I know you've never had this type of relationship before, but if you're always overthinking things, you will psych yourself out, every time. I don't mean to bombard you with all these feelings, expectations, and titles, but I do want you to be my wife eventually. I won't apologize for knowing what I want, and whom I want it with. I love you and if you didn't love me back, you wouldn't be so scared of messing things up. As long as we communicate with one another and cherish one another, there isn't anything we can't do."

"Okay, I get what you're saying. I still need baby steps, Vincent. Otherwise, I can't—"

"I can do baby steps."

"Can you? It's clear you're used to conquering and getting what you want when you want it. This time, though, you're going to have to be patient and give me time to catch up."

"I can do that."

"Okay, good. Now, what are our plans today?" I ask him, and he looks hesitant about something.

"What's wrong?"

"After this conversation, I'm debating whether I should ask you the question I had planned to ask."

"Well, take your own advice, don't overthink it. Just ask me."

"Okay. Uh, do you think some of your fear and insecurities stem from your parents and how you were brought up?"

"I hadn't thought of it, but maybe. Honestly, I never thought about how abnormal my family was until I had something to compare it to— your family. In the time I've spent with you and your family, I saw the way you nurture Junior, laugh with him, teach him, be whatever he needs you to be. Seeing it all firsthand, forced me to realize my relationship with my parents wasn't one built of love. Lately, I've wondered if everything I learned from them growing up is even true. I've been feeling lost because of it."

"Olivia, what happened to your parents?"

"They died. One day, they left me home and went out for groceries and they never came back. After three days of waiting for them to walk through the door, I began to panic. I turned on the television to distract myself when I passed a news channel station. A bridge collapsed, and there were fatalities. I was about to change the channel when one of the cars on the tow truck, completely crushed caught my attention. It was my parents' car. I know it was their car because of the sticker on the back. The reporter stated there were fourteen people who died in the incident, and because they never came back, I assumed they were amongst that group. I've never told anyone that."

"It's okay. I understand. What happened next?"

"Well, I was forbidden to ever go out of the house alone, I was scared, and as far as I knew I had no one else to take me in. So, I learned how to fend for myself. I was homeschooled and I knew enough to get my GED. I was only eighteen years old."

"Well, you can't allow their ghosts to haunt you. You're a good person and you live a nearly sin-free life, despite what you've been told, and despite anything we've done, or will do in the future. I've been curious about your parents, so I kind of did something that I hope you won't be mad about. Just know that I did it out of concern for you."

"What did you do?"

"I had hired an investigator to dig into yours and your parents' pasts."

"Why would you do that?"

"Because I don't think they were your biological parents."

"Wait, what?! Why would you say that? Why would you think that? I know I haven't painted the best picture of them, but you've never even met them. Why would you say something like that, Vincent?"

"I don't mean to upset you, but there's more and I need you to listen to me, Olivia. If there is anything I've learned, it's how lies can spin out of control, and I want to be honest with you."

"Okay, finish."

"Okay, I'll start from the beginning. You told me the day we met that you applied for a position at my company, and you were turned away. After we met, I wanted to know why, and what I found out was… troubling. You were rejected because of your ineligibility, yes, however, that was not the entire reason."

"My company runs an extensive background check on anyone we consider hiring, to prevent corporate espionage, fraud, etcetera. So, the same thing was done for you along with the other applicants. However, it was your birth certificate, and social security card documentation that made you unemployable, even if you did return as an eligible candidate. Olivia, your documents were not authentic, and found to be one hundred percent fraudulent."

"I found it hard to believe that you set out to deceive me because ours was a chance meeting. I didn't see you as a person capable of that kind of deceit, especially when every emotion you feel is transparent. So, I hired you out of curiosity while I poked around into your background."

"At first, I wanted to help you out of whatever danger you seemed to be in by providing a place and honest work for you, but then I began to care about you, and my reasons for investigating you changed."

"Because the documents were such high-quality forgeries, it implicates criminal association and further supports my suspicion that you were given these forged documents for no other reason than to hide your true identity from the world. I have no doubt that the Hunts were not your biological parents, and Olivia Hunt is not your real name. I read up on a few things, and only one thing makes sense. It's referred to as child laundering, and it's when children are illicitly obtained by fraud, force, or funds, processed through false paperwork, and then adopted. I've been listening to the things you tell me they'd say to you, and I know it sounds crazy, but it's the only thing that explains everything."

"That's not it, Vincent. It can't be."

"Think about it, you were home-schooled, you weren't allowed to have friends, and you had limited access to the outside world. I bet you can't tell me anything about your family history, and you've probably never seen a photo of your mom when she was pregnant with you. I would guess there weren't any family photos when you were growing up, because they didn't want any record of your existence."

I pause at that statement, and mentally walk through the bare halls of my old home. "You're right. There weren't any photos anywhere, but that doesn't prove they weren't my parents, or they were trying to hide me for some reason."

"Olivia, one red flag can be explained away, but when you add all this together, you get a distorted image of a family that doesn't seem to be a real family. You're right, it could be something else. That's why you get seek out information. I'm telling you this to say, I want to help you find the truth, whatever it is. This is *your* past and *your* life. If you want me to drop it, I will. But, if you want me to dig deeper, I'll do that too."

"Vincent, you've just told me it's possible I was taken from my real parents and raised by monsters," I say heatedly as I get up and start to pace. "I don't understand how this could happen."

"I don't know, but I'm glad I went with my gut and hired you. I couldn't be happier with how things turned out."

"I'm not sure how to process this information, but if there's even a small possibility that what you're saying is true, I need to know."

"Okay. Well, the first step is to get a DNA test. That'll give you definitive answers. I can get that set up for you right away. This means that if and when we do find your family, you won't have to do anything because the lab will already have your samples. All they will have to do is compare it once they send theirs."

"Okay. Yeah, I want to do that."

"It will be alright, I promise." He says pulling me into his arms.

I feel a ball of lead in my gut. I want to believe him, but if he's right, I'm a complete fraud. How could anything ever be right again?

Chapter Twenty-One

STILL OLIVIA

The following morning, I walked around in a daze. I've just been going through the motions all day. I couldn't recall one thing I ate or drank for breakfast, what we talked about, or anything else. The only thing on my mind were the burning questions: Were the Hunts my parents? Where do I belong? To whom do I belong?

Later that day, after dinner, I grab my computer and go into the library to be alone, but mostly to sit, think, and possibly research. I liked this room from the moment Patricia showed it to us on the tour — it's peaceful here.

I pick a sofa overlooking the garden, sit, stare into space, and let my mind wander. I find myself wondering if there were signs.

I sit up, open my computer, and start looking for the information I need. I research child laundering, profiles of traffickers, kidnappers, and their treatment of the victims, and I find mirrors of my life. Why did I never question their obsession with keeping everything private, never letting me look anyone in the eyes, always looking down, and not being allowed to go out in public by myself?

They had no relatives, no friends ever came to visit us, there were no birthday parties with friends, no family vacations — nothing. I can't remember them talking about their parents or any other family, ever. I always thought that was because they weren't likable people, but could it have been something more? I've known since the deaths of my parents that they weren't great parents or people compared to others, but were they criminals?

If this turns out to be true, then I might have relatives out there somewhere, maybe even parents who've been looking for me all this time. I don't know how to deal with those thoughts, so I close my laptop and go back to staring into space.

"I take it Vincent told you about his suspicions?" Pops asks, startling me. I hadn't even heard him come in.

"Yes, he did." *And apparently everyone else.*

"Are you okay?"

"I feel blindsided and stupid. I've been trying to remember anything significant that happened to me in my early childhood, and I can't. It's just blank. I've been researching the things he thinks happened to me, the profiles of the people who commit the crimes, and I see mirrors of my life. I don't know why they'd go to the trouble of kidnapping me — it was obvious they hated me. I just don't understand what happened, or how I ended up with them. Everything I read about child launderers tells me that if they took me, I was meant to be sold to someone illegally, so why didn't it happen? Why did they keep me?"

"If Vincent is right, you're the victim here. You should be proud of yourself for surviving and being a capable, caring young lady, despite all the obstacles in your way. Your questions are valid, and in time, they will be answered. From what my grandson told me, if you could handle those people for all those years, you can handle anything, including my Vincent."

I can't help but smile at that. "Jury's out on that one, Pops."

"Olivia, you're only the second woman he's ever felt strongly enough about to introduce to me. His heart has been stomped on by the wrong woman, and he's been afraid to care about anyone else. My boy was jaded and closed off, but since he met you, he's been happy, and I think he's ready to take a chance on love again.

"Finding someone who loves you for who you are is difficult for people like us — nine times out of ten, people only want to be around us because they want our money and influence. I'm glad he recognized you were that one out of ten. When you find someone like that, you have to hold on tight and cherish them. I know from experience what can happen if you don't," he says sadly.

"May I ask a personal question?" I ask him.

"Of course."

"You seem to want love for Vincent, a second chance. I guess what I'm asking is why are you so against it for yourself?" When my question is met with silence, I think I've overstepped. "You don't have to answer that." I say, trying to retract the question considering the tension it's causing him. I don't want to cause him any stress, especially in his condition.

Pops runs his hands through his hair and takes a deep breath before responding. "Guilt and pride. I made a promise to my first wife that I'd never love another woman or remarry. When I met Patricia, I couldn't keep one of those promises, and I've been trying to keep my word about the second."

"Okay, so why not just date her in the open then instead of hiding her here?"

"Because eventually she will expect marriage. A woman like her is meant to be someone's wife."

"So, why not yours? I'm new to this relationship stuff which gives me a fresh perspective. Maybe it's time to realize you can have more than one love in your lifetime. Do you really think your first wife wanted you to be miserable, and alone for the rest of your life? Plus, you wouldn't necessarily be breaking your promise because you can never love Patricia the *exact* way you loved your first wife — they're two different women. I think you've suffered enough, and I think it's time to live life in the open and finally be happy."

"You may be onto something, young lady. I do want to fix things — I just don't know how."

"Well, I've listened to how you and Patricia interact, I see the life you had here, so based on that, I have some ideas. Do you by chance have any paintings of Patricia, or anything else you've kept during your time together?"

As a matter of fact, I do, in my studio. While we are on the subject, Vincent told me you like to paint. I want you to feel welcome to work in the studio if you'd like to. I'd also love to see some of your work. I have an eye for talent, and I have connections in the art community. Maybe I could help make something happen for you."

"I paint, but I doubt I have the kind of talent that warrants bothering your contacts."

"Let me be the judge of that," he says as he leads the way.

***

Two hours later, I'm lying awake in bed, thinking about my talk with Pops. Vincent was right, he's an interesting man, and full of character and wisdom. Vincent is blessed to have him in his life. *What would my life be like if I'd had someone like him growing up?*

I hate that Pops is so sad and tormented. I don't think he's ever completely gotten over the death of his wife. I hope he finds a way to come to terms with it so he and Patricia can have the life they deserve.

I'm surprised to find that billionaires have the same problems as everybody else. For some reason, I thought they all lived in some bubble where they all lead happy lives and get exactly what they want.

I also thought all parents were like mine until I saw something different. I now know that parents aren't supposed to be intentionally cruel and resentful. While no family is perfect, the unconditional love and support for one another is something to cherish, and a beautiful thing to see. To be on the receiving end of that kind of love would be a dream.

"Are you awake?" Vincent asks, turning his body to spoon me.

"Yeah, I am."

"What's on your mind?"

"It would be more accurate to ask what's *not* on my mind. I can't seem to turn off all the thoughts circling around in there."

"How was your talk with Pops?"

"It went well, really well. He's great, you're lucky to have someone like him in your life."

"Yeah, he always knows just what to say when you feel like the walls are closing in on you. When I used to get countless 'return to sender' letters every time I tried to write to my father, he always knew what to say to me to keep me from spiraling.

He has a way of putting stuff into perspective, for everyone but himself it seems."

"Why did your father leave?"

"Well, without my mom, he didn't want to be a parent. I don't think he really knew how to, either. He had the exact opposite reaction that Pops did when my grandmother died. Pops pushed through, he raised my father, and always strived to be the best at everything — even a fictitious designer for his startup company, as we just found out. My father, on the other hand, checked out of life and shirked all his responsibilities — including me."

"You were lucky to have someone who always put your feelings and needs first. My parents made me feel like I was a burden like they were doing me a favor by doing the little they did do for me. I guess now I know a little bit more about why things were that way."

"We don't know for sure yet, but it's likely. Also, I hope you realize you have someone in your life who will always put you first now. There's nothing I wouldn't do for you."

"I'd do anything for you, too."

"I just want you with me, always. Loving you comes as second nature to me."

"I can't wait to see what that's like. I've never had that from anyone before," I say as I turn to face him, and plant a soft kiss on his lips.

"Do that again," he says, and I do. Then he kisses me back with so much intensity I practically melt in his arms.

"Don't worry. I'm going to make you forget about everything for a few hours. Trust me?"

"Yes…with everything I've got," I say, and I mean it.

"You won't regret it," he says as he proceeds to do deliver on his promise.

Chapter Twenty-Two

STILL OLIVIA

The next week flies by and it's filled with laughter, fun, and togetherness. I'm able to enjoy the people around me, and forget about my problems, and the pandemic. It's a welcome break.

I know I'll remember this trip fondly, because it's the first time I've experienced being part of a family, having real friends, and being a cherished girlfriend.

I close the door to Junior's bedroom and head downstairs to have another glass of wine with Patricia. The wine she's introduced me to probably cost more than my old apartment's monthly rent, but it's delicious, and I'm going to enjoy it without feeling guilty.

"So, I guess I need to stock up on a few bottles of this when we get back home, huh?" Vincent asks, coming into the room and picking up the bottle.

"That would be great."

"I bring my girlfriend who has never had a drink in her life until a few weeks ago here, and in one week, she's on her way to becoming a wine connoisseur," Vincent quips, and we all laugh.

"I'm afraid you've got me to thank for that," Patricia says as she raises her glass in a toast. "To the two of you. Make every single day count, hold onto one another, and make love win. To love," she says with a smile that doesn't quite reach her teary eyes as she raises her glass.

"To love!" everyone says in unison. Patricia quickly finishes off her wine and excuses herself.

When she's gone, I look over at Pops and nod my head at him. He gives me a tight smile, and we watch as he excuses himself and goes after her.

When I look back at Vincent, he's giving me a strange look.

"What was that?"

"What?"

"I saw that look between you two."

"I have no idea what you're talking about," I say with mock innocence. Vincent leans in to kiss me just as his phone starts to ring.

"Go ahead and take it, it might be important," I say with disappointment as he answers. Vincent has been getting a lot of work done here, and I can't get in the way of that. I know he's Vincent here, but at work, he is Mr. Taylor with responsibilities, and countless people relying on his leadership.

As he continues his conversation, I let my eyes roam over his handsome profile, and I can't help but smile. He's the kind of man fairy tales are made of; a prince charming came to life, and he chose me.

Chapter Twenty-Three

POPS

I follow Patricia out to the back patio, feeling like the worst kind of scum. *She's hurting, and I'm the cause of it.*

The heart attack was my wake-up call, and I realize that I don't want to spend the rest of my life alone.

I slowly approach her, hoping she will listen to me. "Patricia, I know this is the worst timing, but will you take a walk with me? I want to show you something." I say, feeling even worse when she finally meets my eyes with her sad ones.

"Why? It won't change anything, Vincent."

"You might be surprised," I say as I extend my hand to her. She looks at me for a few moments before taking it, and I know that I can't mess this up. I've got one shot before I really lose her.

"Why are we going to your studio?" she asks after she realizes where I'm leading her.

"I told you; I want to show you something."

"Okay, but I've seen everything in here."

"We'll see." We step into the studio, and she gasps as she sees what Olivia and I have set up.

There are candles and rose petals surrounding the entire room

creating a path that directs us to the paintings I've never left on display, even to Patricia.

One is a portrait of Patricia looking out the window with a smile on her face, and the sadness in her eyes makes the image even more poignant.

The second is a painting from a memory I had of her standing at the stove cooking our first meal in this house. She's laughing, holding a wine glass in one hand and a spoon in the other. She was so happy in this one, and I want that for her again.

I watch nervously as she studies them. "There's more," I say, pulling her further into the room. A few more steps bring us to paintings of her highlighting our years together. It's my tribute to our love.

Fresh tears began to run down her face as she stops to admire each one. When she finishes, she turns to me and asks, "What is all of this?"

It's now or never, I think nervously. "This is me telling you that I love you more than anything and apologizing for making you feel like I was anything but proud to be with you. I'm asking for forgiveness for taking so long to come to my senses and do what's right. Finally, this I me asking with all my heart, will you do me the honor of becoming my wife?" I say as I take the ring out of my back pocket and get down on one knee.

She just stares at me, and I'm preparing myself for a no when she shouts, "It's about damn time!"

I sigh with relief, she gives me her hand, and I slip the ring onto her finger, stand, and pull her into my arms.

"I have a lot to make up for," I say, holding her close, "so we aren't getting any rest anytime soon."

Chapter Twenty-Four

VINCENT

One week later

I'm making use of Pop's home office to take a few meetings, speak with board members, check in with my contractors, respond to emails, and make calls. I have two more calls to make before I can get back to my lady, so I dial the first contact.

"Mr. Taylor." Lawrence greets me.

"Is it done?"

"Yes, I've just filed the documents, and I'm walking out of the courthouse as we speak," Lawrence, my lead company lawyer says. "I handled everything. She agreed to the terms and signed the NDA, so you won't be hearing from Lauren again. She's aware of the legal and financial repercussions if she contacts any of you," Lawrence says.

"Thank you, Lawrence."

"No problem, sir. Let me know if you need anything else."

"Will do. I'll talk to you later." I say as I hang up and dial the man I've been waiting to hear from; Tyler Johnson, the private investigator I hired to investigate Olivia. He picks up on the third ring.

"Mr. Taylor."

"Have you found anything?" I ask directly.

"Yes, actually. I had every intention of calling you today. I called in a couple of favors from a few FBI buddies, and today, they returned with some information. I'm confident I have your answers."

"Tell me everything," I say, checking to make sure Olivia can't overhear.

"The people who raised your friend were named Craig and Tasha Redford. This couple was a modern-day Bonnie and Clyde. The FBI suspects they ran their child-trafficking and illegal adoption ring through Redford Consultant Services LLC out of Connecticut back in the early '90s. They have no way of knowing how long this activity spanned, and they have no idea how many children were involved. The Redford's both had long rap sheets, including arson, kidnapping, child laundering, extortion, and a laundry list of other petty crimes. The FBI has been after them for more than twenty years."

"Is that everything?"

"No. The only reason this couple finally turned up on the FBI's radar was because of a couple who was going through them to handle their adoption. At some point, they began to suspect the Redfords of running a criminal organization and they went to the police. However, they were not caught because they apparently had friends in the precinct who tipped them off. They burned their business to the ground and ran, taking the baby meant for that couple with them, and were never seen again.

"Shit!"

"There's more. There were five kidnappings of newborns in that area — three boys and two girls. The names of the female infants taken were Naomi Miller and Carmen Richards. I believe your friend to be Naomi Miller, but only a DNA test can confirm it."

"Okay, tell me about the parents. Are they still alive?"

"Yes. Their names are Andrea Ellis and Logan Miller. They both work for Southwest Airlines — he's a pilot and she's a flight attendant. They're still together and they live in Los Angeles, California.

"According to the FBI, in all kidnappings, Tasha posed as the nurse that approached the parents during the shift change, hours after they gave birth. She took the babies under the guise of needing to take them for routine tests or shots. None of the young mothers thought twice about handing their child to her, and it was an effective way to snatch those kids without raising suspicion until hours later. Those parents never saw their babies again."

"That's some twisted shit! Those people really were evil. Why are you so sure Olivia is Naomi Miller?"

"Aside from there being only two options, the timing, and the fact that your friend is the spitting image of Andrea Miller."

"Okay," I say trying to process this new information.

"How do you want me to move forward?"

"Reach out to them and tell them you might know where their daughter is, but they must agree to a DNA test before you'll give them any more information. Make it clear that nothing less than a positive DNA test proving she's their daughter will get them in the same room as her. I want them to use the lab Taylor Industrial uses so there's no chance the DNA results can be tampered with. We want to keep all parties safe until we're sure about what and who we're dealing with. The Redfords were well-connected, and even though they're both dead, it's safe to assume the people who helped them will want to cover their asses if they find out what we've discovered."

"But before you call them, I want you to investigate their finances to make sure there were no suspicious payments in the months before the birth. I want you to make sure they didn't benefit from the kidnapping in any way. I want to be doubly sure they're on the up and up before they get anywhere near Olivia. I don't want them to take advantage of her or me."

"I'll get right on it, Mr. Taylor."

"Thank you, Tyler."

"No problem. I should have something to report by tomorrow."

"Okay, talk to you then." I say into the phone before ending the call and immediately call Lawrence.

"Mr. Taylor." He answers on the first ring.

"I need to alert you of some things that are happening. I may need you to draw up some NDAs and oversee something. You are the only one I trust to see this through."

"I'm listening, sir." He says, and I proceed to tell him everything. When I'm done, he makes a few legal suggestions in addition to questions concerning the logistics of carrying out what I've asked of him.

"Olivia and I discussed the possibility that her real parents might still be alive, and she's already had a DNA test sent to the lab. The lab just needs samples to compare it to."

"You'll need to let your HR Director in on this so they can help you prepare you for when the press gets wind of this. It's going to cause a PR nightmare. Some of your board members are already restless, and this might be enough to push them into trying something stupid."

"I appreciate the warning. That's exactly why I trust you so much. I'm prepared for the fallout, whatever it is. My main concern is protecting Olivia, so in the coming weeks, I'd like to set up a trust for her, and I'll need you to draw up the paperwork."

"Okay, just let me know when. I'll be in touch soon."

When we hang up, I make a call to Veronica and have her arrange flights and hotel accommodations for my pilots to come back to L.A. After flying us here, I put them on a plane back home because I didn't know when we'd be returning. Now, I need them to be here, on standby to bring the Millers directly to us when everything is confirmed. *They're her people, I know it.*

As I sat talking with Lawrence, I googled Andrea and Logan Miller, the parents of the kidnapped infant Naomi Miller, and Tyler was right. Olivia is a dead ringer for Andrea, and she resembles her father as well.

Naomi Miller...

This is it. I have the answers, and in doing so, I've upended her entire world. I can't even imagine what misery they have endured all these years not knowing what happened to their baby. Have they been hoping she was still out there somewhere?

The fact that this couple is still together after going through losing their child that way speaks volumes about them. I think these people are Olivia's parents too because she seems to have their strength of character. I can't help but wonder what if I hadn't come along? What if the pandemic never happened? I need to make this right as best as I can, I have to. With that thought in mind, I made one more call.

***

135

An hour later, I feel much better. I've done everything possible to ensure no matter what, with or without me, she will be okay.

"Vincent?" Olivia asks, stepping into the room and closing the door, pulling me from my thoughts.

"That was him, wasn't it? The investigator you told me about?"

"Yes, and you're going to want to sit down. I have a lot to tell you."

I proceed to tell her everything I learned, excluding the purchases and decisions I made on her behalf today. I don't know what reaction I expected, however, calm and logical was not it. It's a lot to process, and I'm not sure she realizes just how much everything has changed. At least now, she knows she isn't alone, and she knows the motives behind their cruelty.

That day, I remained glued to her waiting for the other shoe to drop. However, she genuinely seemed to be okay, so I let my guard down a little, and gave her some space.

Two days after I broke the news to her, I woke up in the middle of the night to find she was not in bed. I hear the shower running and get up to investigate. As I get closer to the bathroom, I hear muffled crying, so I open the door and steam rolls out.

I step inside, not caring that my shorts are getting soaked, and walk over to Oliva. She's curled up, her arms wrapped around her legs, and her head is resting on her knees as she sobs in a corner under the water.

"Oh, honey, let's get you out of here," I say as I pick her up. Her skin feels so rough compared to its usual softness which tells me she's been in there for a while. I push the shower door open with my hip, step out of the shower, and sit her down on the closed toilet lid. I grab the nearest towel and dry her as much as I can before picking her back up.

"Come on, sweetheart, let's go to the other room." I say as I wrap my arms around her and hold her up as I walk us out of the bathroom, to the bed. We sit on the edge, and I hold her as she cries some more. "I know you're hurting, but don't hide from me. Let me hold you and be here for you, baby." I say to her as she holds onto me tightly.

I should have known she wasn't okay. For the first time, she was exceptionally good at hiding how upset she is. I feel completely useless in the face of her pain and sorrow. I can't fix it, I can't throw money at it or make it go away. So, I just hold her and pray exhaustion takes over soon so she can rest.

This is my fault. I'm the one who opened Pandora's box and let out all the secrets. Maybe I should've let sleeping dogs lie.

Eventually, the tears stop completely, and I ask, "Would you like to try to sleep for a while?"

"Yeah," she croaks, her throat undoubtedly raw from crying.

"Okay, you lay down and rest. I'll be here."

All I can think about is how badly Olivia is suffering, and the fact that the worst is yet to come once the media finds out. Still feeling useless, I wrap my arms around her, and I try to get some sleep too.

It's been about an hour, and unlike her, sleep hasn't come for me yet, so I get up, careful not to wake her, and go over to my laptop. I start researching the best ways to support partners who have been victims of abuse, kidnappings, child laundering, human trafficking, verbal abuse, etc. After two hours, I finally climb back into bed and try to sleep again, and I do.

Olivia's scream wakes me from my troubled sleep, and I sit up in a rush. Somehow through the night, we moved to opposite sides of the bed, and she is no longer in my arms. I turn to see Olivia tossing and turning as she frantically mumbles in her sleep. I put my hand on her arm to try to wake her and she feels feverish.

There's a soft knock on the door and I immediately get up and turn the bedside lamp on. "We heard a scream. Is everything okay?" Pops asks through the door. I walk over to it, and let them in, but not before pulling the covers over Olivia.

"No. I think she's sick. She's burning up. I don't know what to do."

"She might be experiencing a psychogenic fever," Patricia says gravely.

"A what?"

"It's when you develop an extremely elevated core body temperature after being exposed to emotional trauma. She was probably pretending she was okay with everything you found out about her past, but her subconscious mind is not handling it well. She needs a lot of emotional support so her mental state doesn't spiral. It would be a good idea to get her to talk to a therapist as soon as possible. She's struggling with her loss of identity, so you will have to be her lifeline," Patricia says with authority.

"I'll be whatever she needs. It's my fault this happened. I couldn't leave well enough alone."

"Or maybe you met her when you did so that you'd be here for her when she needs you. Don't get caught up in blaming yourself for something others did, just keep pushing forward," Patricia says in a mothering tone.

"She'll pull through, Vincent," Pops adds. "She's a fighter. Have faith that everything will be fine."

"What should I do for her right now?"

"Cool her down, keep her dry, hold her, and let her rest."

"Okay. Thanks, Patricia."

"Call us if you need us," she says, and squeezes my hand. That's when I notice the ring.

"You two had gone to bed by the time—" Pops starts when he sees what I'm looking at.

"No explanation needed. Congratulations! I'm really happy for you two!" I say as get up to give them each a hug.

"That's enough of that," Pops says gruffly. "Now, take care of your girl."

The minute the door closes, I start trying to figure out the best way to get Olivia cooled down without disturbing her too much. Eventually, I figure it out, and when I'm done, I climb in and wrap my arms around her. "Don't worry, baby," I say soothingly. "Everything will be alright. You'll see."

Chapter Twenty-Five

STILL VINCENT

For the first time since we've arrived in L.A, I wake up late. The clock on the bedside dresser tells me its nearly afternoon. I look over, and Olivia is still sleeping peacefully. She needs the rest, and I don't want to disturb her, so I get out of bed quietly. I go into the bathroom, brush my teeth, wash my face, get dressed, and head downstairs while taking my phone and laptop with me. I get there to find everyone up watching TV in the living room.

"Is Olivia going to be okay, Dad?" Junior asks when he looks up and sees me standing there.

"She will be. She just needs to rest. She had a fever last night, but it seems to be gone this morning. Sleep might be the best thing for her."

"I've made some soup for lunch," Patricia says. "I thought something simple, and homey might be good for her."

"Thank you. I'm sure she'll appreciate it."

"Dad, come and watch *Black Panther* with us."

"Maybe in a bit, buddy. I need to make some calls first. Maybe we can rent something new tonight and watch it together."

"That would be great!"

"I can order some greasy pizza and we can pop some popcorn and have a junk food fest while we watch."

"Yes!" he says, pumping his fist in the air.

"Pops, do you mind if I use your office for a few hours?"

"Not at all, you know the way."

"Thanks."

"We'll keep Olivia company if she comes down."

"You guys are the best," I say as I head to the office. I've got a full schedule today and I'd like to get everything knocked out as quickly as possible so I can spend quality time with my family.

***

I've been busy putting out one fire after another all day. Now, I'm desperate to get away from work to check on Olivia. However, I need to touch bases with Tyler, Lawrence, and Tina. So, I take a calming breath, and make my first call.

Tyler picks up on the second ring. "Mr. Taylor."

"Are they clean, and have they agreed to my terms?"

"They are and they have."

"Sounds good, let me know if you find anything else."

"Will do." I say hanging up and dialing a number I've come to know by heart. *One more after this.*

He answers on the first ring. "Mr. Taylor."

"They've been cleared by Tyler. Make the call, please."

"On it. I'll get back to you within the hour." He says before disconnecting.

I make my final call, and she picks up on the second ring. "Hello, Mr. Parker."

"Hello, Tina. Were you able to put some listings together?"

"I was. I've already sent it to your email. You can email me which one you—"

"No. I'll look and pick now. I need this done quickly, and I need you to set up a team to get things sorted before we get back to Florida. Let's start with the first one."

By the time we hang up, I feel a sense of productivity I haven't felt since this pandemic began. Just as I'm about to leave the office, my phone rings — it's Lawrence.

"Lawrence."

"I've spoken to them. They will have their samples in by tomorrow morning. I hired a courier to pick it up, and deliver it to the lab here, personally. We should have the results by the end of the day tomorrow."

"What lab are they going to?"

"It's one I recommended. I know the owners, and the lab is known for its discreetness of its high-profile clients. We can trust them."

"Okay. Thank you for this."

"No problem at all."

"Keep me posted."

"Will do, sir."

"Lawrence, you're a good judge of character. What do you think about the Millers when you spoke to them? Are they good people?"

"I think they are good people who have experienced a terrible loss."

"Thank you." I say before ending the call with a small smile and walking out of the office.

Chapter Twenty-Six

OLIVIA

The following day is my own personal hell. Yesterday, Vincent told me that we'd have the results by today, and I have been dreading it. I've panicked every single time his phone rang.

Everyone has been very helpful with trying to distract me, and it works until I hear a phone ring. When it turns out not to be the call we are expecting, I go back into my shell, and they let me. My thoughts are all over the place as I wait to hear my fate. Even if I'm not this Naomi, then who am I? What kind of life am I leading? Is it mine, or someone else's? Why did they have those documents?

I step into the bathroom to collect myself when I hear Vincent's phone ring. I know it's the call we've been waiting for even before I step out of the bathroom. It's something about his voice.

I rejoin him and sit on the bed as he paces around the bedroom and listens intently to what Lawrence is saying. I try to gauge the news by his facial expression, but it's blank and gives me nothing.

"Okay, thank you. I'll get the information to her, and after we've spoken, I'll let you know how we will move forward. I still need you to draw up those documents for me." *What documents?*

"Right away, Mr. Taylor." He says before ending the call and turning to me. His face says it all.

"So, the Hunts were not real or my parents." I say, and it's a statement.

"That is correct."

"Tell me everything he said, Vincent."

"The results say there's a 99.9% chance that you are Naomi Miller, the daughter of Andrea and Logan Miller."

Chapter Twenty-Seven

VINCENT

The next hour goes from relatively bad to relatively well. On the bright side, she has a family who loves and wants to know her. On the other, her entire life, everything, her name, age, birthday is a lie. That's some serious trauma, and she needs to face it eventually.

"Olivia, what do you want to do, sweetie?"

"Please, don't call me that. I can't go by that name anymore, but I don't want to go by Naomi either. That's part of the problem — I don't know who I am! Just… call me Liv."

"Okay…Liv, what do you want?"

"I want to know who I am, where I come from, what kind of people conceived me. The only way I'm going to get those answers is by meeting my biological parents, the Millers. Will I have to wait for this pandemic to end? I haven't even been paying attention to what's going on with travel restrictions."

"Lucky for you, I have."

"I've already made the arrangements. They'll be in Florida by the time we get back. They just have to be cleared by the COVID testers. I've made reservations for them at the boutique hotel just down the highway from the house."

"How did you know I'd want this?"

"Someone suggested I should put myself in your shoes. I knew if it was me in your position, I'd want to meet them right away."

"Thank you, Vincent. That's exactly what I want."

***

I feel like shit. I started this by digging into her past. But now that it's done, she wants to learn who she is and where she comes from, and I want that for her too. I'll be there for her every step of the way, no matter what.

I watch as she drinks wine and laughs with Patricia. She's an amazing woman, and she will get through this. The question that worries me the most is if I will be with her or admiring from the sidelines.

I step on the back patio and overlook the pool as I place the call to Lawrence to let him know how we want to move forward, and we agree on the best way to do it. Lawrence confirms that he's drawn up the necessary NDAs, as well as the trust documents.

"Thanks for everything, man."

"Don't thank me yet. Have you spoken to your HR director? He's pissed you're making him work, and he's out for blood. Good luck with that."

"Yeah, thanks."

"On another note, do you have any recommendations for a therapist who specializes with this kind of trauma? She's hiding it well, but she's having a hard time."

"No, but I can get a list together for you."

"I'd appreciate that."

"I'll email it to you. Is there anything else?"

"No, that's all for now. And, Lawrence, remind me to give you a bonus for all this extra non-work-related stuff you've been doing for me lately."

"It was my pleasure, Vincent. This is life-changing news for several people. It's nice to be a part of making it happen." He says before disconnecting just as Pops joins me on the patio.

"Everything okay, son?"

"No. None of this is okay. She's thanking me now, but what happens when this all hits the media, and they connect me to her? What if she can't handle it?"

"You are both fighters. So, fight for what you want and don't stop until you have it. She's one in a million, and she loves you and Junior. Just be patient and supportive. Give her everything she needs, and it will all work out," he says before leaving me with my thoughts and going back inside. I watch as he stands and watches the apparent twister game that's begun in my absence.

Chapter Twenty-Eight

OLIVIA

I grab my new laptop, the first thing I bought after I started working for Vincent and turn it on. I'm going to do my own research on Andrea and Logan Miller. I Google their names and instantly dozens of videos from CNN, the *New York Times*, FOX News, and NBC pop up. One stands out above all the others, showing a woman crying with a man holding her protectively while he blocks the cameras with his other hand. *These are my parents. They look so devastated.*

They're swarmed by reporters pushing microphones in their faces. The headline reads: "Mother of Kidnapped Baby Naomi Breaks Down on Camera!" I watch the clip, and it brings me to tears.

No one has ever shed a tear over me in my life, but here are people I don't even know crying because they lost me. I can't process how I feel about this. *Twenty-three years! I've missed being loved by these people nearly my entire life.* I scroll down a little further on the search page and see pictures of baby Naomi —

me. I'm so angry, but there's no place for me to direct that anger because the people who did this to me are dead!

I click on every single one of the links about the case for the next hour, finishing with a story about the case being closed ten years ago. The last thing the Millers ever said on camera was, "Naomi, wherever you are, we love you and we will never stop praying for your return."

I close the laptop and fall back against the pillows, crying. It's just so hard to believe. The Hunts weren't my parents!

A short time later, the bedroom door opens and Vincent walks in. "Olivia?" He comes over to the bed and lifts me just enough so that he can slide his arm around me, I lean against him and cry some more. I don't know who I'm crying for, the Millers, me, the time we lost— it's just too much.

"Is this what you wanted Vincent? To pick me apart, find all my secrets, and solve all my problems so I'd be forced to rely on you?" I ask, my voice breaking.

"I know you're hurting, but I know you don't believe that. You wouldn't be here with me if you thought that. Please, don't push me away." Vincent pulls me into an embrace, even though I'm trying to physically push him away.

"This pain hurts so bad."

"I know it does sweetie."

"What do I do?"

"You're facing it instead of hiding or running away. You're already doing it Liv. Just remember, everything will get worse before it gets better, and I'll be here every step of the way. There are a few things I'd like to discuss with you."

"What?"

"I want you to have this. I know it won't fix anything, but it will help. I know it's against your nature, but please take it anyway." he says, handing me a folded piece of paper. I unfold it and gasp. It's a check for $500,000.00.

"That should cover tuition at any school you decide to attend. I can also provide letters of recommendation, and anything else you may need."

"Vincent, this is too much. You know I can't—"

"I know, but I *need* you to take it. I've turned your life upside-down, and for that I am incredibly sorry. Take the money and do something that's completely for you. This could be a new start and it's time for you take charge of your life." I look into his eyes, and for the first time he's ever seemed unsure of himself.

"Okay. When you put it that way, how can I refuse? But I don't know how to manage this kind of money. Will you help me, Vincent?"

"Of course."

"Thank you," I say one more time as I kiss him soundly, hoping to entice him into giving me what I want—him.

"Oli— Liv, no. Not like this. I feel like I'd be taking advantage of you when you're vulnerable. I can't do that. I want our first time together to be something special."

"Vincent! Really? This again? It will be special, and you are not taking advantage of *me;* I'm taking advantage of *you.* Now, kiss me Vincent…please." I say, and that's all it takes for him to lose control.

He pulls me into a slow, deep kiss and maneuvers me over to the bed. He sits down on the edge, and I straddle him and start to move my hips awkwardly until I find a rhythm that works for me. It must work for him too because he closes his eyes and groans. I can see he's still holding back.

I decide nothing is going to happen until I take control, so I whip my shirt over my head and reach to unfasten my bra when he stops me.

"Are you sure about this?" he asks earnestly. "I don't want you looking back on tonight with regret."

"I want you. I want to feel something that's not loss, pain, or numbness. You're the only one who can make that happen. Show me how much you love me, and I promise you, when I look back on this moment, it will be remembered as nothing less than special.

With those words, his hesitation and doubt vanish, and he gives me the most erotic kiss. It's different from any of the kisses we've shared in the past. It's more intimate somehow and it makes me yearn for him with every fiber of my being.

He finishes the job I started and unhooks my bra as I continue my crotch-grinding dance. When he bends and takes one of my nipples into his mouth, the sensation is so intense it nearly overwhelms me.

I look down, lock eyes with him and it's so hot. I feel my orgasm building and I began moving faster against the hard length of him. Just when I'm about to peak, he stops me.

"Slow down baby, we have all night. There's no need to rush. Why don't you stand up and let me take the rest of those clothes off?" he says in the sexiest voice. He undresses me, stands, and does the same.

All I can do is stare. His body is every wet dream and more. In fact, I don't think my dreams, or my wildest imagination could have come close to doing him justice. "You're so beautiful, Vincent."

"So are you."

"I want to make you feel how you make me feel, but I don't know how."

"That's what you want right now, to pleasure me?"

"Yes."

"Do you trust me?"

"You know I do."

"Okay, I'll show you a way both of us can have the kind of pleasure I gave you before. Do you want to try it?" he asks.

"Yes."

"Okay. I'm going to lay on the bed, and I want you to climb on top facing away from me and position this wet, tight, little pussy right above my face." He says, taking his hands and swiping his fingers over my slick folds. "This position will place your face, mainly your mouth right above the place I want you the most. I want you to be on top so that you always have control. You control what happens, okay?"

"Okay."

"Okay, I'm going to lay down."

I watch as he lays flat on the bed and waits for me. I walk over to the side of the bed, near his head, swing my legs over his head, and try to line myself up with his mouth as he instructed.

"Yes, just like that," he says, but I'm too focused on the very erect penis lined up with my mouth. I study it for a moment and notice the drop of silver liquid at the top. "Feel free to explore." He says, so I do, by swiping the liquid leaking from him with my tongue wanting to taste him. "Shit, Liv!"

Loving the control, I grab his penis and stroke it the way he taught me to in the shower when I feel him hook his arms under my lower body, pull me to him, and starts licking and sucking on my flesh. I squeal, and his dick jumps in my hands.

"Sorry about that. He's just excited and wants you to give him a kiss," he says, chuckling.

His tongue licks a trail of fire, then he sucks on me slowly and my legs begin to shake. I want to give him pleasure too, but what he's doing is so distracting.

When he takes a slight break, I quickly take him into my mouth. His gasp is almost sexier than what he's been doing with his tongue. Almost.

I take my time, circling my tongue around his shaft. It's an odd sensation, both hard and velvety soft at the same time.

"Wrap your hand around it firmly and move it up and down," Vincent practically begs, "while doing what you're doing with your tongue."

I do as he instructs, and he seems to get even harder in my mouth, and a moan escapes his lips. I love that I can do this to him.

"That's enough of that," he says in a strained voice. "It's your turn again."

I soon forget about making him moan because I can't concentrate on anything except what he's doing with his tongue. He's literally feasting on me. Suddenly, the pressure builds until it's too much and it crests, bringing me wave after wave of pleasure.

"Oh, my God. That was amazing," I gasp out when I can talk again.

"That was sexy as hell! I want you to do it again," he says as his tongue dives back in. As he thrusts his tongue in and out at a fast pace, I can't hold it in anymore and I scream, then say, "Vincent, someone will hear."

"Don't worry, no one will hear anything. These walls are thick, Junior is asleep by now, and Patricia and Pops are in their own world probably doing the same thing," he says as he goes back to attacking me with his impossibly thick and long tongue. My next mind-blowing climax is so forceful I almost pass out.

"Move your hips baby, ride me face." Hands grab both hips and began to move me in a slow torturous tempo against his tongue. I start to feel that pressure again, and my legs tighten around his head. Vincent begins to move his tongue faster, taking me higher and higher until I burst.

"I think maybe you're ready for me now," Vincent says after the lingering aftershocks which left me limp. He kisses my mound one more time before flipping me over, spreading my legs, and climbing on top of me. He positions his fully erect member at my entrance, and immediately all doubts and fear about what's about to happen have left me; all I feel is anticipation. I know he won't hurt me, and I want this with him.

"This is your last chance to ask me to stop," he says seriously.

"I want this — I want you. Make love to me, Vincent."

As his name leaves my lips, I see him lose the last thread of control and he slowly pushes into me.

The intrusion is so foreign that I tense up, a little fear trickling back in. Vincent bends and takes my nipple into his mouth, circling, nibbling, biting, sucking, I arch my back to meet his mouth, and he thrusts forward impaling me. I gasp at the intense combination of pain and pleasure.

He pauses and looks at me and I smile up at him, reassuring him I'm okay. When he begins to move again, my body reacts, and I start to move with him. I can tell he's trying to take it slow, but I can feel that lovely pressure building again, and I want to see what it feels like when he loses control.

Sensing my need, he begins to move faster and thrust harder while I wrap my legs around him. Our movements become frenzied, each of us working toward our shared goal.

I'm so close that when he growls, "Come on it," that's exactly what I do. As I start coming undone, I feel him following right after me. I swear this time I can see the fireworks.

Vincent collapses on top of me, and both of us are panting.

"Is it always like that?" I ask with wonder

"No, but it will be for us. Love makes all the difference." he says sincerely, and I believe him.

Chapter Twenty-Nine

VINCENT

Despite everything, the last few days have been surprisingly peaceful. Everyone is in a good place, and everyone has had a great time being here, so much that I began to feel like we are in a bubble.

So, imagine my surprise when I open an email from my company's public relations director with an attached link to an article titled *"Taylor Industrial Heir in Romance with Employee Who Forged ID."*

Just the name of the title has me sweating, but not for me, for Liv. This is only the beginning; how will she take this?

I click on the link, and instantly my panic and concern over what's being written about Liv have transformed to feelings of betrayal. As I skim the article, I realize I had every reason to worry because this article is a smear campaign:

> An anonymous source has informed us that Taylor CEO Vincent Jared Taylor III hired a domestic worker who had forged papers. Taylor, who was aware of the fraud, then moved this

employee into his mansion to care for his son, gave her thousands of dollars, and granted her access to his bank accounts.

Has the Taylor heir been allured by a siren's call? More importantly, how will his choices reflect on the company he recently just took public? Is the company in capable hands?

I slam my laptop closed, pick it up, and go find Pops to show him the article. I pace the floor as he reads. "Pops, this is bullshit! I'm afraid this will be too much for Liv to handle. She's not ready for this!"

"I know, son, but the reality of it is she will have to get ready. From now on, she will always be in the public eye, and not only just for her connection to you. She needs to learn how to deal with it. Remember what I told you; she's a strong woman, she will be fine. You both will need to learn how to handle this as a couple. It's just business to these people, and you cannot take it personally. Right now, it's time for damage control. Get the head of the PR department on the phone and tell them it's time they start earning those huge salaries we pay them."

"There's something else, Pops."

"What is it?"

"I know who the leak was. Only one employee knew about the bank accounts."

"Well, I'd say someone's about to lose their job. There are some lines that just can't be crossed without repercussions. Handle your business, son."

"Yes, sir."

I walk away from my conversation with Pops with a heavy heart. I don't want to deliver this news to Liv just as she's beginning to come to terms with everything. Now, I have to once again pull the rug out from under her feet.

I go up to our room and find her in the bathroom brushing her hair. "Liv, honey, we need to talk."

"What's wrong?" she asks as she walks over to the couch in our suite's sitting room.

We both take a seat and I show her the article on my phone. I can see she's struggling to stay calm as she reads, but I see her reaction to the comments.

"Who would give this information to the media?" she asks, her shaky voice betraying her distress.

"It was my assistant."

"Why would she do something like this?"

"I don't know, but I'm going to find out right before I fire and possibly sue her ass. She signed an NDA and a contract— she's not allowed to disclose any personal or company information to the media or anyone else. She violated both by leaking this to the media. Unfortunately, we need to head home immediately so I can handle this. I'll have to meet with my PR department as well as the board and do damage control. Pops and Patricia are staying here for now. So, it will just be us going back."

"What about my par — the Millers?"

"This doesn't change those plans. They are more than welcome to come to visit us in Florida. If you want, I can make the arrangements."

"I do want you to, yes."

"I'll do that immediately. Look, I know this is a lot, and I'm sorry about all of it, the impending media frenzy, as well as the comments. What I don't want you to do is blame yourself or take it to heart, they don't know us, and they damn sure don't know our story which means they can't judge us. Okay?"

"Okay," she says with resignation. "When do we leave?"

"Tomorrow morning. We'll take the plane and pilots who were meant to bring the Millers here after the results confirmed that they are who we think they are. I'll speak with the pilot right now and have him set the flight plan. You should take a hot bath and get your rest. Tomorrow will be a long day for us all."

"Okay, but Vincent?"

"It's all going to be okay, right?"

"It will, I promise." I say, reassuring her with a smile I don't feel before leaving her to her bath and rest.

Chapter Thirty

VINCENT

It's eight in the morning, my alarm is going off, I only managed two hours of sleep, and when I did sleep, I slept like shit.

I gave a promise to Liv last night that I'm not sure I can't keep. I don't know what we are walking into when we get back home. A feeling of melancholy hits me hard when I realize our time of living in this happy bubble has come to an end.

I can't help but feel like I've caused all this turmoil in Liv's life, even though I never intended for things to spiral like they have. I *will* fix it, though — as much of it as I can anyway.

With that in mind, I get up and jump into action. We have three hours until our flight, but there's so much to accomplish before then. First thing's first; I'll get Junior up, fed, and squared away before waking Liv. After a family breakfast Patricia woke up early to prepare, and lots of hugs and goodbyes, Liv, Junior, and I headed to the airport. We're going home.

***

Hours later, we land and Reece, one of my longtime drivers, opens our doors, and loads our luggage into the car. Within minutes, he's back in the driver seat, and we are off.

We arrive at the house to find a media circus waiting for us outside the gates. Thank God the windows on the limo are tinted and the reporters can't see who's inside. That would just make the feeding frenzy worse. When I look over at Liv, I see the terror in her eyes as she looks at all the vultures waiting to pick at our bones.

I make a snap decision and hit the intercom. "Reece, could you get us out of here and take us to this address," I say as I lower the partition and hand him a card.

"No problem, sir," he replies, reversing out of the driveway and heading away from all the journalists.

"Where are we going?" Liv asks nervously.

"Somewhere safe. Don't worry. We're not going to deal with the reporters today, but eventually we will have to."

Fifteen minutes later, we pull up at our intended destination. I reach into my briefcase and pull out the remote my realtor shipped to me along with the keys, paperwork, and deed. I hadn't planned on bringing Liv here yet for fear of overwhelming her, but I think it's the best hideout for us right now.

We pull through the gates, and I click to close them behind us. The car follows the winding driveway up a hill, and I see, my latest purchase sitting there waiting for us.; a brand new 2022 Nissan Murano.

Reece pulls up beside it, and I notice that Junior is leaning against the car window completely knocked out. The driver immediately gets out to unload bags, and I turn and look at Liv, put my finger to my lips signaling for her to be quiet with a nod toward Junior, and motion with my head for her to join me outside.

We get out and I close the door softly. "Can you give us three minutes?" I ask walking to the driver.

"Yes, sir. Take your time, he'll be fine."

"Thank you." I say smiling. Loyalty is key, and I thank God for all the people who have been loyal to me over the years, including Reece.

"Where are we," Liv asks, as we walk up to the door together, hand in hand.

"Come walk with me and I'll explain." We reach the front door, and I put in the code to retrieve the key my realtor left in a box hanging on the knob. I unlock the door and we step inside, leaving the door open.

"So, you bought another house just in case we'd need a hide-out?" Liv asks as we approach the door.

"No, Liv. This is not my house, it's yours. That car in the driveway is not mine, it's yours, too."

"*What?* What do you mean it's mine?!"

"I had my realtor start looking for houses the day I found out about the Redfords, and I made an offer on this house the day after I found you in the shower."

"But, why? Are you kicking me out? Are you breaking up with me?"

"Liv, of course not. You're welcome to stay with me as long as you want."

"Then why did you do this, Vincent?!"

"Liv, please hear me out. I know you don't like taking anything you feel you haven't earned. I also know my wealth is intimidating and maybe a little overwhelming for you. I just wanted you to have a safe haven that belongs to you. I mean, I kind of made it so you don't have a place to live unless you live with me, so I wanted to give this to you so you can make this home yours.

"The deed to the house and the title to the car are in your name — your real name. I know you don't want to go by that name right now, but I had to use it for it to be legally yours. The

deed and title are in the envelope on the counter in the kitchen."

"This is too much. I don't understand why you're doing any of this."

"I'm doing it because I want you to have some independence, should you ever want it. Doing this for you means you won't have to rely on anyone ever again. I'd rather you be with me, but if you change your mind, you'll be taken care of. So, please, please, please, don't fight me on this. Just accept it so I don't have to worry about you," I say to her, lifting her chin so I can look into her eyes.

"Thank you, Vincent. Thank you for everything," she says with tears rolling down her face.

I look down at her and smile. "You know, the press and my assistant weren't far off. There's nothing I wouldn't do you, there's no mountain I wouldn't move for you. Thank you for coming into my life and showing me that trust, sincerity, and happiness are possible, even for a man like me." As I bend to kiss her, I can see she's smiling for the first time in a long time. All I'm feeling right now is sweet relief.

"You realize this is overkill, right?"

"Well, go big or go home, right?"

"I guess." She says slowly, looking around.

"Liv, I have more money than I could spend in three lifetimes. I wanted to do this for you, so I did. Please don't focus on the price tag. Despite popular opinion, money isn't everything

Plus, this house was meant for you. It has a huge room with great light that would make the perfect place for your art studio."

"I don't think I'll ever get used to the way you are with money. But, I know you were trying to do something nice for me — so, thank you."

"You're welcome. Now come on, let's get Junior up, get our luggage inside, and explore," I say as I lead the way.

Five minutes later, and it's just us three in this unfamiliar house. Junior is up, but he's cranky, so we lay him down on the couch and let him fall back asleep.

"Thank God it's move-in ready, or else we'd be making pallet."

"Wait, the furniture is all mine too?!" Liv asks with excitement in her voice.

"It is, but feel free to change, do anything you want to make it your own."

"I don't want to change anything, I love it!"

"My realtor Tina will be happy to know that. So, is that a yes to us staying here a few days until the dust settles? It might be one of the few places the reporters won't think to look for us, for a while."

"I've never had house guests before. I think I like the idea already."

"I'm a house guest? So, does that mean I have to sleep in the guest room?"

"Don't be ridiculous. In fact, I think we should have a special celebration to christen the house later tonight," she says with a sexy smirk on her face.

Chapter Thirty-One

VINCENT

After the grand tour, we all get settled in and then explore the food situation. I'm glad I had the sense to ensure the pantry freezer and fridge was all stocked with everyone's favorites. Liv decided to cook spaghetti, and it was delicious.

After we finish eating, Junior went off to play video games on his phone while I help Liv clean up.

"So, what's the plan?" she asks.

"Why are you so sure I have a plan?"

"You always do."

"Well, there isn't much I can do about the reporters swarming the house. All we can do is wait it out here, if that's okay."

"Of course, it is. *Mi casa es su casa,* literally. So, shut up with asking my permission already. You know I want you both here."

"I just want to be sure. I've kind of unleashed hell on earth for you in more ways than one. I just want to make sure that I put you in the best position to fight it."

"Vincent, you did turn my world upside-down, but you also freed me. I've always been constantly worried that I'd somehow end up being everything that they said I was or worse, like them because I grew up with their influence. Now that I know what kind of people they *really* were, I can stop feeling like a bad seed. I'm not like them. From what you've told me, I come from good people. How can I resent you for that? Besides, you know the truth always comes to light. You were just the flashlight I needed to show me the way."

"You know, you're one of the strongest people I've ever met. I hope your real parents turn out to be everything you've wanted and more. Even if they're not, you always have me, Pops, Junior and Patricia.

"I appreciate that. I have a feeling I'm going to need you all. So, what do we do now?"

"Well, you can still meet the Millers whenever you want. The decision of when is all yours. Take as much time as you need to decide. I still have a little work to get done today, so we can discuss it further when I get back, if you want. But, Liv, I've read up on stuff like this, and you're going to need more than just my help and support to get through this. So, in the bag with the deed, you'll find a list of therapists who specialize in this sort of trauma. If you want to talk to a professional, look through the list, research the doctors, and decide which one you like best."

"That was very thoughtful of you. Thank you, Vincent. I'll look it later. Right now, Junior and I have a serious Mario Kart battle to wage. Go, handle your business. We'll be fine."

"You sure?"

"Yes. No one knows we're here."

"Great. I'll make it quick. You'll hardly know I'm gone. Mind if I take your new ride?"

"Seriously? You paid for it. Feel free to drive it any time you want. I can't drive it anyway because I don't have a driver's license and I don't know how to drive. So, I'm afraid you've got your work cut out for you, sir."

"Looking forward to it," I say, laughing. "I'll be back soon."

***

Once I got to the car, I punched an address into the GPS, reminding myself to thank Lawrence again for the overtime he's been working. The gates opened and I pulled out of the driveway. *The car rides like a dream! Liv is going to love it!* I think, feeling like a teenager driving his first car. That feeling is quickly overshadowed by the thought of what I set off to do.

Thirty minutes later, I'm parked in front of my soon-to-be ex-assistant's house. I get out, go up to the door, and ring the bell. Shortly after, an annoyed Veronica opens the door and I ask coldly, "May I come in?"

"Wow. The big boss is making a house call. This should be interesting. Come on in," she says a bit sarcastically. I look around after coming through the door, and see her home is cozy and neat. This house is nicer than what I expected, considering the neighborhood.

"What brings you by, Mr. Taylor?"

"You know what brings me by, drop the act. I'm not interested in playing games."

"Okay, then. What do you want?"

"I want to know why you did it. How could you leak details about my personal life and company business to the media?"

"After what you did to me, you ask me that?! You picked some bitch off the streets, hired her, moved her into your house — which I've never even been invited to visit by the way — and then you gave her access to your money by making *me* set her up as an authorized user instead of doing it your fucking self!! How dare you? You knew how I felt about you!" she practically screams at me.

The rage behind her words has me at a loss. "I have never done anything to suggest that I know of your so-called feelings for me or returned them. That's on you, not me. I see this isn't going to go anywhere, so, I'll make this short—"

"I'll make it shorter. Fuck you and fuck your company too! You don't appreciate or deserve shit! I waited five fucking years for you to admit you wanted me, and instead you give everything to some tramp off the streets! She can't do anything for you — that's my job! So, I no longer give a shit and yes, I decided to make some extra cash for my trouble. I'm done caring about you. Now, get the fuck out!"

"I'll go, but I'll say this. I didn't fall for a tramp; I fell for the woman I'm going to marry."

"*Marry* her? Wow, she must have some magical pussy to trick you into that. I've never so much as seen you go on a third date since I've known you, and now you're Christian fucking Grey. What a joke! Just get the fuck out."

"You're fired as of right now. There will be no severance pack-age — you violated the terms of your contract. If you have any questions, you can contact human resources. You are not to step foot on any Taylor property, and you are not to come within 500 feet of me, or anyone else in my family." I say before walking over to the door.

"Oh, I won't be coming near you again. Go and run home to your little damsel in distress. It won't last long, I *guarantee* it!" she yells as I walk back to the car.

Wow. How did I not notice that woman's obsession? She's fuck-ing insane! I think as I hit speed dial for Lawrence before I even start the car. "Hey, I need you to do something for me ASAP," I say as soon as he picks up.

"Sure, boss. What is it?"

"I need a restraining order against Veronica. I don't want her anywhere near anyone I care about. Make it cover every property and anything else you can think of."

"I take it things didn't go well?"

"Ha! That woman is bat-shit crazy. She was pissed about me being with Liv because she thought we had a romantic relationship. I've only ever spoken to that woman at work. Hell, we don't talk at all if it isn't work-related!"

"Maybe we should keep an eye on her. Better safe than sorry."

"Yeah, I think you're right. Do it."

The whole drive back to Liv and Junior, I think about the rage I saw in Veronica's eyes. I'm afraid her vendetta against me is far from over and Liv will end up being a casualty. I can't reconcile that unhinged person with the meek and ever-helpful assistant I thought I knew. I guess I need to start paying more attention to what's going on around me instead of always having my head buried in my work.

I dread having to tell Liv there's even more drama coming her way. I don't want her to be overwhelmed by all my baggage and go running off in the other direction, but at this point I'd understand if she did.

When I get back to Liv's house, I find her and Junior asleep on the couch in front of the TV. I smile and savor the feeling of coming home to this scene. This is something I thought I'd never have.

I walk over and pick Junior up so I can carry him to bed. I'm not going to be able to do that much longer, he's getting big. As I start to walk away, Liv wakes up and I say, "I'll be right back, I'm going to put him to bed."

"Okay," she says groggily.

"We need to talk," I say when I come back. I sit down on the couch beside her and pull her close.

"I hate when you say that. It always means something bad. Do I need another glass of wine for this conversation?" she jokes. When I don't laugh, she looks expectantly at me.

Reluctantly, I tell her everything that went on with Veronica, and amazingly she just says, "It's okay. We'll work through it together."

"I'm sorry about this, and about everything else that's disrupting your life."

"It's okay. Really. You can't control other people, and I know you meant well when you uncovered what the Hunts did, so stop apologizing, please. I don't blame you."

I pull her to me and kiss her as if our lives depend on it. Then, I scoop her up in my arms and head upstairs to our bedroom. I make love to her with the knowledge that my days with her might be numbered, and it breaks my heart.

In the middle of the night, my vibrating phone wakes me up. By the time I find it, I've missed the call. I unlock it and see that I've missed multiple. There are eight voicemails, ranging from the company's head of PR, Lawrence, and several from unknown numbers. I go to the head of PR's message first, and see a link attached.

My instincts are telling me that this is what Veronica meant when she said, *"It won't last long, I guarantee it!"* Apparently, her revenge campaign has begun.

Taylor Industrial Heir's New Woman Revealed!

It has been discovered by DNA tests that the love interest of billionaire Vincent Taylor III, CEO of Taylor Industrial, is a child laundering victim named Naomi Miller. Miller, who had been living under the name Olivia Hunt for more than 25 years, was allegedly abducted by launderers who posed as her parents until their untimely deaths.

Taylor and his new woman were spotted pulling up to Taylor's residence earlier, but they left the scene before answering any questions.

As I finish reading this latest bombshell, I add the hiring an overtly hetero male assistant to my "need-to-do" list. At least that way, I can be sure as shit something like this won't happen again. *Fuck! I hate this complete truth stuff,* I think as I roll over, wake Liv up, and let her know the latest bomb that's gone off in our lives.

One week later

Today's the day Liv meets the Millers. I can see she's bursting with nervous energy, so I volunteer to pick them up from the hotel after my meeting with Lawrence, the board, and my public relations director. That way, she'll have some time to compose herself, but I have ulterior motives. I'd like the opportunity to check them out for myself before I let them anywhere near her. I'll protect her from anything that can hurt her, and that includes the Millers, and myself.

I take some time to reflect on what the press has said about me as a businessman and a person as I make the drive. What I hate the most is the pot shots they take at Liv left and right. I don't think there's been one article that paints her in a good light, and they don't even know the true nature of events. At this point, I'm considering a defamation of character lawsuit on both our behalf.

The Millers aren't faring much better. They told me the media's been calling at all hours, hounding them for comments and interviews. It's sad they can't enjoy the fact that they've finally found their daughter without having to deal with all this chaos of my celebrity thrown in.

I'm glad Liv decided to invite them to her house. For one, it would limit the media's access to us all, and secondly, anywhere else would've been too impersonal. I've done a good job of keeping the media from finding us so far, but chances are they will at some point.

I'm here at Miami's private terminal, sitting in the car as I watch the plane push in until it rolls to a stop. I wait until I see the door being opened before leaving the car to greet them. A few moments later, I see the Millers deplaning the company jet, and I am at a loss for words. This couple looks young and very attractive. As they get closer, I get my first up close look at Andrea Miller, and she's gorgeous. She and Liv look more like sisters than mother and daughter, but the resemblance is definitely there. Logan Miller looks healthy and young, but his haunted eyes tell another story.

"You must be Vincent, Nao—, Liv's boyfriend. The man who made all this possible," Andrea says as she approaches me and gives me a hug, while Logan holds his ground, assessing me.

"That would be me," I say sheepishly.

"Thank you. You have no idea how long we've hoped for this day. This is my husband, Logan," she says, as he steps forward, and I shake his hand.

"It's nice to meet you both, and there's no thanks necessary. I'm just glad I could help," I say, noticing Logan is still watching me suspiciously.

"You must care deeply for her to go to these lengths to find out what happened to her, and then find us," she says and I smile knowing she can see what's written all over my face.

"Yes, ma'am, I do."

Logan abruptly turns and walks away to help the attendants unload their luggage from the plane, and I follow. When we finish, Andrea's bubbly excitement has convinced me that they are genuine. For whatever reason, Logan is not as transparent, but I don't expect him to be. In his shoes, I'd probably act the very same way, especially after all the things in the newspaper painting me and their daughter in a bad light. Whatever his problem is, I'm sure I'll find out eventually. He doesn't seem like the type to keep quiet for long.

"Shall we go?" I ask, as I hold out the door for them.

"Yes, please. We've waited long enough. Let's go meet our daughter." Andrea says with nervous anticipation as they both get into the truck.

Chapter Thirty-Two

OLIVIA

I sit looking out the window, waiting for the Millers, I can't help thinking about the drama-filled, television worthy life I have been living. I'm now known to the world as a gold digger. *Me!* The crazy thing is, I'm being trolled based off Vincent moving me into his house, and allegedly giving me access to bank accounts. *Again, me!* What happens when they find out about the money, the house, and the car! I'll be crucified!

They've found out who I am, and I'm sure they know the implications, yet I am still being drug through the papers for all the world to see. I can picture the title now, "*A gold digger or a victim.*"

This is a mess, and I don't think things will be getting quiet for us anytime soon. I've tried to do as Vincent said, but it hurts to have so many people who don't know me publicly tear me apart.

I've done my best to put the media and their attacks on my character out of my mind, but it's challenging sometimes. In the grand scheme of things, the general public's opinion is not import-ant to me, but today is. My greatest worry is that what they've read will influence the impression they have of me, and they'll be disappointed.

I see the car pulling through the gate, and my anxiety multiplies tenfold. Suddenly, I'm on my way to a full-blown panic attack. But, before I can go completely down that rabbit hole, I feel a hand on my shoulder.

"I can hold your hand if you want me to. Dad says that calms you down," Junior says, and I smile even as tears roll down my face. I've never had anyone care for me the way Junior and Vincent do. It's the best thing I've ever felt.

"You're right, it does," I say, taking his hand. "C'mon, let's go greet our guests."

"We're back!" Vincent yells as he comes through the door carrying bags. "They're on their way in." he says as he sees me and Junior.

"Okay."

"I'm going to go ahead and take their luggage to their room, so you can have a moment alone with them."

"No, stay, please. The luggage can wait. I need you here."

"Then here is where I'll be," he says just as they appear in the doorway.

My eyes land on the woman first because seeing her is like looking into a mirror. She must've been equally surprised at seeing me because she just stops and stares at me.

Finally, she breaks the spell. "Vincent told me you were beautiful, but he didn't mention the resemblance. You look just like me when I was your age," she says, struggling to control her emotions as her lips tremble.

"I can see it too," I say, not quite sure what else to say. After a pause where I just keep staring at her, I realize I'm being rude and say, "Oh, I want to introduce you to Junior, Vincent's son." I unclasp his hand and put my arm around him, more for moral support for myself than him.

"Junior, these are…the Millers."

"Hi," Junior says shyly.

"It's very nice to meet you, Junior. I know we're going to become great friends," Andrea says, getting a smile out of him.

I look behind her to see Logan Miller standing in the doorway watching everything unfold. I glance over at Vincent, and it's like he's reading my mind.

"Junior, I think Pops is expecting a call from you. Why don't you go call him while we get the Millers settled in?"

"Okay. I'll tell him you all said hi."

"Good deal," Vincent says as Junior grabs his cell off the counter and leaves the room to go make his call.

I take Vincent's hand and squeeze it to give myself strength, and I notice Andrea do the same. "I just wanted to get this out in the open right away. I'm sorry for everything that happened to you, to us. I know what the results say however, I'm not ready to be Naomi Miller. I know that's probably what you want most after all these years, but I don't remember anything from that time, and I don't have any connection to that name as of right now. However, I do want to get to know you and be a part of your lives and I hope you feel the same way. I've never had loving parents or a real family, but I want one. I hope that's enough for now."

When I finish, they smile at one another, and "It's enough," simultaneously comes out of both their mouths before they pull me and Vincent in for a tight hug.

Now that I have a closer look at Logan, my dad, I can see some of my features come from him too, which is surprisingly pleasing. The way they look at one another is so beautiful to see. I'm glad their love stayed strong as they weathered the storm of losing a child. That tells me everything I need to know about them. They're nothing like the people who raised me, and that alone is enough to make me want to be a Miller.

Vincent's ringtone sounding breaks the spell of the moment. He looks at caller ID and says, "It's the head of public relations. I'm sorry, I need to take this. I'll be right back."

"Okay," I say uncertainly, totally freaking out. *What if I say something wrong?*

"Why don't you give them a tour of your home?" he says, and I can tell he doesn't want to leave meaning the call is important.

"Yeah, okay. I can do that. Go ahead and take your call."

"Thanks babe," he says as he leans in and pecks me on the cheek before walking in the direction of the backyard before accepting the call.

"Okay, are you ready for the grand tour?" I ask with more enthusiasm than I feel.

"Lead the way," Andrea says.

I look at Logan, but he's watching Vincent's retreating back with a less than friendly look on his face. "You two go on without me. I want to speak to Vincent about something once he finishes his call. Go ahead, I'll entertain myself until he finishes up," he says pasting on a fake smile compared to the very genuine one I just saw.

"It's okay. Let them talk, so we can spend some time together," Andrea says pulling me in the direction of the stairs.

When I look back worriedly in Logan's direction, she says, "They'll be fine. He just needs to be a … dad. We've waited a long time to meet you. He won't do anything to ruin this day, I promise."

"Okay," I say as I lead my mother up the stairs and give her a tour of my home. *Now that's something I never imagined I'd be doing.*

Chapter Thirty-Three

VINCENT

I'm so glad Liv understood how important this call is. I thought this matter could be postponed, but apparently it can't. The volume of calls I'm receiving tells me it's spun out of control, and Liv will have to know about it soon. This is yet another bit of drama to pile onto the stress she's already feeling.

I'm agitated as hell as I walk to the back yard. I saw the look Lawrence sent me this morning when they mentioned the most recent allegations against me.

Apparently, some cousin to the mover I punched wants their fifteen minutes of fame and went to the media about the altercation. I woke up to emails and texts about him appearing on a popular TV show that was set to air tomorrow, and I'll be the main topic.

This is a big day for Liv, and I'm not going to ruin it for her by bringing up fallout from my jealous actions.

Just as the call is about to go to voicemail, I answer with a curt, "Hello."

"We need to talk," my PR director says with irritation.

"Yes, we do. You can't inundate me with calls and emails every time my name comes up in some story or soundbite. Do the job that we hired you for."

"Have you heard about the latest episode of the *Sandra K Show*?"

"I have. You sent me a link."

"But you didn't respond to that or any of the other messages and emails I've sent. Look, I wasn't hired to clean up the fallout from your personal life. I'm Taylor Industrial's PR director, not the agent for your billionaire saga. If this continues, you're going to have worse problems than too many voicemails from me," he says and promptly hangs up on me

What the fuck? Does this guy not realize I'm his boss? I'm totally pissed off as I go to my contacts and hit the speed dial for the HR director.

"Hello, Mr. Taylor. How may I be of assistance?"

"I want you to set up a severance package for our current public relations director, find an interim director, and then pull all the records for everyone who's applied for that position over the past five years. We need someone with experience working for a company as big as ours. I want to do virtual interviews with the people you choose. I'm afraid you'll also have to hire a temp to act as my assistant. I fired my old one.

"Get it done right away — end of the day today or by Monday. Oh, one stipulation for the assistant position — they must be married, over forty, and they need at least 20 years of experience."

"I'll get it done."

"Thank you. I'm sorry to dump all this on you with no warning. Watch for a bonus in your check this month as well as an extra week of vacation."

"Thank you, sir! I'll get it done right away." I end the call and immediately call the snotty ex- PR guy back.

He answers on the first ring and says, "Are you calling to tell me you finally realized how dire the situation is?"

That statement is greeted by silence on my end. I get the impression the dumb fuck is expecting an apology.

"Hello? Are you there?" he asks irritably, and I smile because I'm going to enjoy this.

"I understand the situation perfectly," I say, just to fuck with him.

"Annnnd?" he prompts.

I assume this is where he thinks I'm going to kiss his ass and tell him I'm sorry I was short with him. *God, this man is an ass-hole.* "*And,* I'm the face of the company. If I have a problem, then the company has a problem. Dealing with those problems is your responsibility, since you're *head* of PR. What is *not* included in those responsibilities is you calling me and whining about every-thing you're having to do to accomplish your job.

"You work for *me.* Therefore, *you* do not tell *me* what to do. So, in conclusion, since doing the job you were hired to do is appar-ently too difficult for you, it's time for you and Taylor Industrial to part ways."

"You can't fire me! Who's going to clean up this mess you've made? *You need me!*"

"Therein lies the problem. You think you're irreplaceable. I hate to tell you this, but I can replace you by the end of the day. You're nothing special. There are a ton of people who would kill to have your job — and they'd do it without whining and pissing off the person who pays their salary. To prove I'm not a complete monster, your severance package is being prepared for you as we speak. Goodbye, Mr. Anderson," I say before ending the call.

I go back to my messages and click on one of the links the ass sent me titled: ***"Businessman or Criminal?"***

Good morning, fellow Floridians! Whew, I don't know about you, but I woke up with questions on my mind, so let's get to it. Today, we're discussing our favorite, sexy and scandalous billionaire, Vincent Taylor III. A source has come forward saying one of their family members was assaulted by the billionaire himself. This relative was then paid off and forced to sign a non-disclosure agreement.

Doesn't this strike you as criminal behavior? If all criminals were as loaded as this guy, none of them would ever be convicted!

Wondering what made him lose it like that? It's none other than his notorious damsel in distress, the modern-day Cinderella, Naomi Miller, formally known as Olivia Hunt.

"Stop listening to that garbage," Logan says from the patio door. "It'll just piss you off. Mind company?"

"Sure," I say.

I walk over to the bar under the veranda, take out two tumblers, and select a single malt whiskey from the cabinet. After pouring the drinks, I walk over and plop down in one of the empty chairs, then slides a whiskey over to him.

"Thanks."

After I down my drink, I simply wait him out. He obviously has something on his mind.

"Did you like the tour?"

"No, I decided to give them some alone time so you and I can get to know one another."

"Okay. What do you want to know?"

"There are a few things I don't understand. You seem like a capable young man. You run a billion-dollar company, and you're intelligent. You could have any woman on this planet. So, why do all of this? Why hire her, bring her into your home with your family, give her money and access to you and money that's yours when you knew she was not who she presented herself to be? What exactly does her position entail to deserve everything the press says you've given her?"

"Don't tell me you believe everything the media says."

"No, but how could we not pay attention, knowing what we know now?"

"Excuse me?"

"You heard me. How did you benefit? Because no matter which way I flip it, I can't tell who's taking advantage here."

I'm annoyed by the offensive questions, but what irritates me more is him insinuating this when he should be spending time getting to know Liv. She doesn't deserve his suspicion. He doesn't even know either of us. I don't take this shit from anyone, and I've bent over backwards to make sure hin and his wife have a good first impression of us both.

"So, what is it you want to know, exactly?" I ask coldly. "Are you asking me because you want to know my intentions toward your new-found daughter, or are you indirectly questioning my intelligence by insinuating that a CEO of a billion-dollar company that employs thousands of people can be fooled into giving away his money? I can't figure out where you're going with this, so I suggest you put your cards on the table."

"I want to know everything."

"First and foremost, I know this is a difficult situation — for everyone — so I'll cut you some slack. I know you don't know me and don't really have a reason to trust me, but I brought you and your daughter together, and I don't have ulterior motives for doing that. I just want Liv to be happy.

"I get that you want to protect your daughter since you couldn't when she was taken, but I'm not the villain in her story, and I never will be. I won't defend my relationship with her to you, but I will tell you that I fell in love with her the moment I saw her. She's everything to me, and I'd never abuse her trust.

"The only thing that matters to me is her — what she wants, feels, and thinks. I'm here to support her, no matter what she chooses. She's a strong, resilient, beautiful woman and she doesn't deserve that kind of accusation — especially from you. She's already dealing with it from the media. So, as a favor to you, I'm going to forget this conversation. A re we on the same page now?

We stare one another down for a few seconds before he blinks and sits back. "Okay, fine. That's fair. Just so you know, you can't protect her from everything. I know the frustration of wanting to protect those you love from anything that can hurt them, but you can't always do it. Also, secrets can be dangerous. You should tell her whatever you've been keeping from her."

"I tell her everything, always. I just wanted to give her today before I dump this new media story on her. She deserves this time — you *all* do. It's one thing to have your world turned upside-down by discovering you were kidnapped at birth, it's another for every newspaper and talk show host to be calling you a slut, disparaging your character, and speculating on every aspect of your life because of the man you've involved with."

"Look, I had no right to question you after all you've done for us … I was wrong. I just wanted to do what I should have done all those years ago — protect her. Not being there for 25 years haunts me. We finally find her, and everything she's supposed to be getting from her father is coming from you. *You're* her protector. I guess I let jealousy, ego, and pride take over. I can admit when I'm wrong. I'm sorry, Vincent."

"It's already forgotten. I don't matter, she does. You two wouldn't be here if she didn't have room in her heart for you.

She wants both of you to like her. The psychological damage the Redfords did was substantial, but it didn't break her. She's strong, and she's managed to stay kind, humble, and innocent despite her upbringing. She's amazing. If you give her the chance, she'll prove it to you."

"You know, I didn't know what to think of you after we found out you were involved with our daughter. I realize now that I'll never get the chance to meet the other guys she dated to interrogate, and scare the shit out of them, and I'm kind of disappointed. I just want you to know that I approve of you. I hope one day soon, you'll be a part of my family," he says with a smile, shocking the shit out of me.

"It would be a privilege, sir."

"The name's Logan," he says, and inwardly I sigh in relief.

"Alright, Logan."

"Okay, now that we have that settled, I think we both need another drink," he says, and we both laugh.

From this point on, it was like the previous conversation never happened. I'm guessing a huge weight lifted off his shoulders once he got the answers he needed. I understand his need to protect his daughter — I'm a father and I'd do anything to protect Junior — even from his birth mother.

Speaking of the devil, I haven't heard a peep from Lauren. I'm not surprised, since Lawrence is brilliant and completely thorough with everything he does. At least we don't have to deal with her along with the media circus.

"You're thinking too much," Logan says. "C'mon, let's join the ladies before we both end up in the doghouse," he adds, instantly reminding me of Pops. In that moment, I knew we would all be okay.

Chapter Thirty-Four

OLIVIA

As it turns out, Andrea was right. By the time we come back downstairs, Vincent and Logan are talking and laughing like they're best friends. The tension I sensed earlier is completely gone.

"I told you everything would be fine," she says, noting where I'm looking. "He just needed to make sure things were okay for you, like any other father would. Unfortunately, it's kind of late for that — you already know how to protect yourself. We've missed so much," she says, fighting tears.

"You're both here now, and that's what counts."

She takes me by surprise and hugs me. When she pulls away, she grabs my face and just looks at me. "Your dad gave you the dimples, but you have my mother's eyes. When I look at you, I see so much of us. You're breathtaking, Liv."

"Thank you. I guess I get it from you. Tell me about your mother. Is she still living?"

"No, honey, she passed away five years ago from a heart attack. I know she would've loved to be here to meet you."

"What about Logan's parents?"

"They're still with us and they live in Burbank. His mom has dementia, and his father takes care of her."

"Oh."

"His father knows we're here with you, and he would love a chance to meet you sometime soon. Maybe you can come visit us? I can schedule it if you'd be interested."

"I'd like that very much."

"Well, we'd love to have you," she says as we walk over to the couch.

I'm not used to playing host, but finally remember my manners. "Would you like a glass of wine or water?"

"A glass of wine would be lovely," she says. "Wait, before I forget, I want to give you something." She removes her enormous Guess purse from her shoulder, sits it on her lap, and retrieves a manila envelope.

"What's this?"

"It's your birth certificate. Vincent told us you might need it. You'll have to have it to request your Social Security card and get identification. It's no pressure, but at some point, even if it's not Naomi, you have to be somebody to move forward."

I pull it out of the envelope and stare at it for several long seconds before remembering what I was about to do. "You stay there, and I'll pour us some wine."

I take the time while I get the glasses and bottle to get myself under control. When I feel less shaky, I open the bottle, grab some glasses, and head back to where she's waiting for me.

"Here you go," I say setting the glasses on the coffee table and pouring each half full. "It's hard to believe all of this is real. I didn't realize I would feel so…I don't know. Lost, maybe? For as long as I can remember, I've been Olivia Hunt and now I'm suddenly someone I don't even know."

Andrea surprises me again by grasping my hands and saying, "I know meeting us at this point in your life is probably strange beyond words, but I want you to know we have every intention of being a part of your life, if you'll let us. We don't care what name you use, only that you're alive and well.

"We didn't lose a name that day, we lost you. It's okay if you don't want to be called Naomi Miller. We'll love and cherish every moment with you regardless. How about we just take it one day at a time? Would that be okay?"

"Yeah, I think that sounds good," I say as I take a sip of wine.

"Besides, the way Vincent looks at you, and the look you look back tells me you might be changing your name again soon anyway. I love to see it, how happy and in love you are. He's a good one, and it's clear he'd do anything for you. When I see you two, it takes me back to when Logan and I were young. I don't know how we managed to stay together through everything and make it to this day, but I'm so thankful we did. I hope the love you and Vincent share is just as strong as ours."

I can't even look her in the eye. "No, Vincent loves someone who doesn't exist, so I don't see that happening for us."

"He loves *you*, not your name — and that's the only thing that's changed about you. You're still the same person he fell in love with. Trust that. On days when you doubt everything else, trust that. It will take you to places you never thought you'd see."

"Thank you," I say as I hug her, and it feels exactly how I wished it to; like going home.

Chapter Thirty-Five

OLIVIA

The next three weeks with us all under one roof go really well. We get along so well that you'd think we'd always known each other. Apparently, Andrea had something called FMLA that allowed her to take almost the entire month off work, and Logan had a lot of sick time accrued. Whatever the reason, I'm glad they could spend time with us.

Logan, my dad, is quiet but sweet. I can tell he's working on opening up more, and I'm trying to be patient. He still won't tell me what he and Vincent talked about that first day though. Eventually decide to leave well enough alone on that front, since they're getting along so well now.

Junior adores them too, and Andrea dotes on him. She's an open book, and I love her for it.

The media is still looking for us, but we all ignore that problem for the time being and enjoy our time together. Not only did I think I'd ever have this, I never in a million years expected to be grateful for having my identity ripped away, but I am. I want these beautiful people in my life from here on out.

That's what makes today so bittersweet — their going home. Though I'm trying to fight it, I feel like I'm being abandoned all over again, which is illogical. Yet, it's how I feel as I watch Vincent and Logan load the luggage into the car from the window.

"Hey, are you okay?" Andrea asks from behind me, giving my shoulder a gentle squeeze.

"I'm trying to be."

"Hey, this is *not* goodbye. You know you're welcome at our home anytime. You can also call us when you need something or just want to talk. We're not going anywhere," she says, wiping away the tears slowly rolling down my cheeks. "Come here, give me a hug," she says, pulling me close, just as Logan and Vincent walk in.

Amazingly, they see us, and understand what I need and join in on the hug too. This is love — something I've been missing my entire life.

"Okay, the jet lands in fifteen. We've got a little time to get there because they have to refuel, but the window is getting tighter by the second," Vincent says, as we all wipe tears from our eyes.

I'm so thankful for him. He's been my lifeline, and he's gone above and beyond to make this a good, memorable time for us all.

"You guys need to get going. I'll be okay," I say to everyone, and I can see in their eyes that I look the opposite of okay. "Please call me as soon as you get home."

"We will."

"FYI, ladies and gents, the hounds will be on us the minute we arrive at the terminal. Someone tipped them off that we have a company jet being refueled on the ground bound for L.A." Vincent says with irritation.

"That's our cue," Logan says, and everyone hugs one last time.

"See you soon, Liv. We'll call as soon as we get home."

"Thank you, Andrea and Logan, I- I love you," I say, and they come hurrying back to pull me into their arms, smiling like I've always dreamed my parents would at me — lovingly.

"We love you too. We've always loved you," Andrea says, and I feel like this is truly the beginning of my real life.

We finally pull away from each other, and surprisingly I actually *do* feel okay. "Have a safe flight, you two," I say, and watch as they walk out the door again. Suddenly, I've made my decision and before they get too far, I say, "One more thing. You can call me Naomi from now on."

They're shocked into silence, and I run out and hug them both again. I look back and see Vincent watching us with a smile on his face.

***

I'm sitting on the couch watching *Hercules* on Netflix when Vincent gets back from the airport. I'm glad I didn't go with them. I didn't want to give the media vultures anymore to pick over, plus I've hit emotional overload today. It was much nicer having our goodbyes in private and then having a little time to myself so I could get myself together with no one watching.

"Hey, come and watch the movie with me," I say. When he remains where he is, I know something's up.

"I have a question for you."

"Okay, what is it?"

"Is your decision to be Naomi Miller permanent?"

"Yes. I hadn't decided until that very moment, but I meant it."

"That's amazing," he says with a smile that doesn't reach his eyes. "I'm really happy for you."

"Vincent, what is it?" I ask with real fear in my heart that something isn't right.

"We need to talk." *Even I know that's not good.*

Part 2

I am Naomi

Chapter Thirty-Six

NAOMI

Nine Months Later

It's been almost a year, and Vincent has been true to his word about me walking this path alone. It hurts that he's stayed away for so long, even though I knew he would after he told me his intentions.

After Vincent left, I didn't want to leave the couch for days. My worst fear had happened — I was completely alone again. He said I needed to learn who I was without interference from him and all the media attention he attracts, and I was so angry with him for leaving me that way. It was no piece of cake working through the anger and heartbreak.

I came to grips with it eventually and I decided the first step to reclaiming my life was taking back my name back. I had to wade through a lot of paperwork to make it official, but I got it done with the help of the Miller's. I'm now in possession of non-fraudulent copies of my Social Security card, driver's license, and I have a passport.

What I did find out is that, even without him in my life, everyone's eyes were on me everywhere I went. It had become my new normal and being Naomi Miller did nothing to dim the media spotlight.

I had a difficult and bittersweet road to self-discovery, but therapy has helped me through it all, mainly knowing I'm worthy of love. Regardless of the resentment I felt towards Vincent, the milestone meant more because I did it myself.

My parents have been there by my side the whole time. I even moved in with them because I just couldn't stand being alone in the home Vincent bought for me. It was too depressing. I haven't been back since I moved.

I've also had a chance to meet the rest of my family. Doing that was the final missing piece to the puzzle that is Naomi Miller. It helped me heal the rest of me. I now know exactly who I am and where I came from. I'm finally at a place where I can truly say I'm whole. That's certainly a blessing.

Currently, I'm on a plane headed to one of Pop's vacation homes for Patricia and Pop's wedding. I've been anticipating this day since Patricia called me six months ago and asked me to be her maid of honor. I was the only female who she knew that knew about her and Pop's relationship, and she heard from Pops how I helped him. So, she said I'd earned the title.

I couldn't say no to her, even though I knew it would be painful for Vincent and I to be around one another and not think about what could have been.

All that effort to stay away from me, and today, he has to see me. Needless to say, I've gone all out for the occasion.

"Flight Attendants, prepare the cabin for landing." The captain announces, shaking me from my thoughts. The rest of the flight flew in the blink of an eye. The moment I step off the jet bridge,

my anxiousness goes on high alert. This is my second time flying commercial alone, though I technically didn't have to because Patricia offered to send a jet. I refused because that's not who I am anymore. I want the experience of the journey and all that comes with it.

I've come to terms with being Naomi Miller, and I hope they'll embrace me as I am now. Granted, my name, my looks, the way I dress, the way I think have all changed. But, I'm still me, just a more evolved version. Yet, I'm worried and all the insecurities I thought I'd left behind are coming back full force.

Claiming my bags and picking up my rental car goes surprisingly quickly. By the time I make it to the hotel the guests are staying at, I've got about half an hour before I have to be at the rehearsal dinner.

The moment the door closes behind me as I step into my hotel room, I drop my bags by the door and walk into the bathroom. I look in the mirror to make sure I don't look as on edge as I feel, especially near other wedding guests, or Vincent.

I have intentions of going down to the hotel bar, drinking wine, and relaxing. It will feel good to unwind before I face the people I'm terrified to see, but whose presence I've been missing for almost a year now.

I take off my travel clothes, change into a bodycon day dress, unpack my bag, and hang my clothes. I went all-out for this trip. I waxed everything, got manicured and pedicured, bought lingerie, and some new dresses because I want to look irresistible. I chose a sexy red cocktail dress and black Christian Louboutin heels for tonight's dinner — the dress acting as my "armor" so I can get through the rehearsal. I get everything set out so I can enjoy maximum relaxation time before coming back to get ready.

I'm anxious to see what everyone else thinks about the changes I've made — especially Vincent. I smile, hoping he'll love my new confidence as well as the toned body my trainer has been torturing me to achieve. Even feeling confident in who I am, I still need a little liquid courage.

So, I throw some heels on and head down to the bar to order a glass of Riesling. I get settled at the bar, order, and in minutes my nine-ounce glass of wine is placed in front of me.

I'm just about to take my first sip when I feel a tap on my shoulder. I swivel on the barstool to see a beautiful woman smiling at me expectantly. Instantly, I smile back.

"Naomi Miller, right?" She asks and immediately my smile disappears. *Is she a reporter? How does she know who I am?*

"Yes. And you are?" I ask, coldly.

"Wow, you look different from the pictures on TV. You look stunning!"

"Thank you. I'm sorry, I didn't catch your name."

"I'm so sorry! I'm Patricia's first husband's daughter, Cassie Vergez."

"Oh, wow, it's a pleasure to meet you," I say, smiling at her, and momentarily dropping my guard.

"Oh my God! I am being so incredibly rude. I completely forgot to introduce my date," she says.

I look behind her and can't believe who's standing there. "Vincent?" I ask breathlessly.

"Hello, Naomi. It's nice to ... formally meet you," he says, extending his hand.

"Meet? You're his former housekeeper, aren't you?" she asks sweetly, her question oozing with sarcasm.

Okay, now I'm pissed. "Yes and no, but you already knew that right Callie?" I say, throwing the incorrect name out as I meet her gaze unflinchingly.

"It's Cassie."

"Be that as it may, don't let me stop you from enjoying your … date." I say, trying to get this obnoxious woman as far away from me as possible.

"You know what? Patricia has been singing your praises for weeks, and I'd love a drink. Besides, we need a little girl time before the rehearsal. Don't you think?"

"Not really, but apparently you think we do," I say with no warmth in my voice.

"It's settled then. Babe, I'll catch up with you later."

"Are you sure?" Vincent asks, but he's not talking to her.

"Don't worry. I can handle a little … girl time." I say confidently. He looks at me one last time, taking in every inch of me, before walking away.

"Can I get a gin and tonic?" Cassie asks the bartender as she takes a seat beside me. She turns and smiles at me, and I just stare at her expectantly, which seems to give the results I'm wanting. "You're still in love with him, that's cute. I can understand why, he's a powerful, accomplished man. Be that as it may, I think maybe it's time you forget about him. I hope you don't have any hopes to renew your … friendship because I am here with him, and he's *mine*. Besides, what man in his right mind would want anything to do with all the baggage you have? He's done enough for you, so don't expect anything else. I'm in his life now, and I'll be the one he marries. He's moved on to bigger and better things."

"You know what? It'll be fun to watch you learn just how wrong you are. I have no doubt no one, including me will be the reason you and Vincent fall apart; it'll be you. You're obviously threatened by me, and I can understand why. I'm the woman he actually wanted and fought for. You're an acquired taste and he likes women that are cut from a different cloth compared to spoiled, leeching bitches who just want him for what he has and who he is. I'm afraid you don't make the cut. You're stunning to look at, but he'll see through that. Vincent outgrew women like you a long time ago."

"I love Patricia, but that doesn't mean I have to like you or put up with your snide comments about me and my life. I'm here for her, and I won't be intimidated by you. So, in the future, you should refrain from 'girl time' with me. I've been taking boxing classes and I'm more than willing to demonstrate what I've learned if pushed. Enjoy your drink, Ice Queen," I say as I drain my glass, throw a fifty on the bar, and walk away without another word." *What a bitch!*

That whole scene annoyed me, so I headed back to my room to collect myself before getting dressed for the rehearsal. As I search in my clutch for my room key, I hear someone coming up behind me. My instant goosebumps, and his aftershave tells me who it is before I even turn around.

I slowly turn to meet Vincent's eyes, and I smile. I don't care what's happened, I've missed the hell out of him and it's good to see him, but he doesn't need to know that.

"You've changed," he says with wonder in his voice. "You look fucking amazing, Naomi! I didn't think you could be more stunning, but I was wrong."

I say nothing, but on the inside, I'm doing my happy dance. Yes, this is exactly the reaction I wanted, but I wanted it in public. I hadn't prepared to be ambushed this way.

"So, what happened to 'girl time?' he asks when I don't respond.

Finding my voice, I say a bit snidely, "Well, two minutes of conversation with your 'date' and I wasn't feeling too social anymore. What do you want, Vincent?"

"I just wanted to apologize. What she said is *not* how it is between us."

"You don't ever have to apologize for something someone else says or does. I know you've moved on, but I hope you wouldn't been taken in by a woman like that again. She's no better than Lauren," I say, and he laughs.

"Are you so sure I've moved on at all?"

"It doesn't matter, Vincent. Well, if you don't mind, I need to relax, freshen up, and get dressed for the rehearsal."

"Can we talk please? Preferably, not out here in the hall?"

I look at him for a second, before opening the door, stepping inside, and motioning for him to follow.

"You have five minutes, talk."

"So … how are you? How's your life? How are your parents? I want to know everything."

"You couldn't be all that curious. You haven't contacted me in nine months."

"Naomi, please don't do that. You know why I did what I did."

"I do. You decided you knew what was best for me and that I couldn't handle things myself, so you did it for me. Your God complex is not attractive at all, Vincent."

Chapter Thirty-Seven

VINCENT

Fuck! How does this woman do this to me by just looking at her? I haven't seen her in months, but my dick and my heart jump at the sight of her. I almost didn't recognize her at the bar, which made me wonder how Cassie knew exactly who she was. When I realized she wanted to gloat about being my date, I thought I'd have to step in to protect Naomi. However, after eavesdropping on their conversation, it was apparent I wasn't needed. Apparently, Naomi can handle herself and doesn't need rescued, which is sexy as fuck. Not only did she not back down, but she handled Cassie like a pro. It was amazing to watch. When she left the bar, I had to follow her.

I guess Pops was right about her being stronger than I gave her credit for. For once, I'm happy to be wrong. I can see I made the right choice by giving her the time and space let her come into her own as Naomi.

Now it's time to start groveling and reclaim my love's heart seeing as she has obvious resentment. "You're right, Naomi. I realize now you're stronger than I gave you credit for, and I was wrong. I know I hurt you, and I'm sorry for that. But don't think

that because of what I did, you're the only one who's been hurting. I miss you. I think about you every day."

"Yet you walked away, which makes it hard to believe what you're saying."

"It wasn't easy, believe me. I was afraid you'd end up resenting me if I stuck around and interfered while you were trying to figure out who you were. I knew I wouldn't be able to resist interfering, so I took myself out of the picture for a while."

"It was my decision, not yours. I still needed you and you did exactly what I always thought you would; you left me behind."

"I know that now. I didn't mean to, just wanted to put your well-being before my wants. I wanted to be with you, but not at the expense of you finding yourself and getting to know your parents. You deserved that time without complications from me, and I had to give it to you."

"Well, I guess it's all water under the bridge now. I know you had good intentions, but just remember that you don't know everything," she says, throwing her hands up. *Oh, hell no! This isn't hopeless and we aren't fucking done!*

"I need another drink. Will you join me for something from the minibar?" she says as she walks over to the mini-fridge and bends to grab two beers out.

"That depends on whether a drink is all that's on the menu," I say as I eat up the mental and physical distance she's put between us. *Fuck!* Seeing her bent over in that dress with that ass has my dick hard as a rock. She looks so good, I'm not sure I can control myself.

"What do you mean?" she asks coyly, as I step behind her and place my hands on her hips.

"I mean I haven't seen you in forever, and now you're right here in front of me looking so good … Did you do this on purpose? Do you want me to go crazy?!" I say as I rub her ass.

"Nope, divine intervention at it's best." She says with amusement in her voice.

"You know what? I *do* want a drink, but not from the mini bar — from *you*." I say as I inhale her fragrant scent.

"You're mighty confident for a man who came here with another woman."

Being this close to her, I can smell her perfume and the scent that's purely hers, and it's driving me crazy. "Well, I'm not sure the woman I wanted to bring would want to speak to me. I had to take the scraps. Beggars can't be choosers." I let that hang for a second, then lean in and kiss the back of her neck. She doesn't pull away or slap me, so I do it again.

All I can think about is getting her naked, and I need her on the same page. I reach up and move her hair to the side to unzip the sexy form-fitting dress and she doesn't stop me. Once unzipped, I slide the dress straps from her shoulders down to her hips. I turn her to face me and I drink in the sight of her in a sexy red lace bra that makes my mouth water. I slide my hands up and under her bra, massage her breasts until she whimpers. Needing to see her, I reach around her and unclasp her bra. I stop and step back to admire her beautiful breasts before bending and sucking on one nipple.

"What do you want me to do, Naomi?"

"I—" I cut her off by sucking her other nipple into my mouth and grazing it with my teeth.

"I've missed you. Will you let me show you how much?"

"Yes, Vincent, please." She says in a sultry voice. I push her dress down to reveal a lacy thong, making my fingers itch to take them off. I pull them down quickly, she steps out of them, and they join her bra on the floor. I get on my knees and pull the rest of the dress down to reveal her sexy matching thong. In seconds, I pull them down and she steps out of them, and I begin to kiss her stomach and pelvis, teasing her. She's close when I swipe my tongue between her sweet pussy lips before picking her up, laying her on the bed, and spreading her legs.

Jesus, that's a beautiful thing to behold! I dip a finger between her pussy lips and find she's wet and ready for me. I slide my finger back and forth, earning more moans. I add another finger and she start to come undone. I keep going, but she quickly grabs my hand and holds it in place.

"Vincent, please, stop teasing me," she begs me.

I reply "I might, if you do something for me."

"What?"

"Tell me you've missed me."

"I did miss you idiot — every single day."

"Then show me how much, Naomi."

I wasn't sure she'd accept the challenge, but she surprises me by taking my hand out of her pussy and licking my drenched fingers and boldly looking me directly in the eyes while doing it.

"Shit! That was sexy as fuck!"

"That's not all I can do with my mouth," she says boldly, as she pushes me on my back and climbs on top of me. She grabs my dick at the base and licks the tip nearly causing me to cum instantly. When she looks up at me and starts to stroke me the way I taught her before deep throating as if her life depended on it, I almost lose my shit.

"Okay, I changed my mind. You can wait to have your fun with me, but not until I have you every way possible. Any objections?"

"None."

"Good, come to the bottom of the bed, and get on your hands and knees turned away from me." I say as I get off the bed.

She does as I instruct, and I pull her hips up so that her ass is in the air and smack it before gently pushing her back and head down flat to the mattress. "Put your hands behind your back."

Again, she complies and closes her eyes, trusting me completely as I take off my belt and use it to bind her wrists. "Is that okay."

"Yes, I'm fine." She says, reassuring me. I then take in the scene in front of me as I kick my shoes off, take my tie off, cover her eyes, and tie the material at the back of her head.

"Don't move.

Looking at her like this makes me want to fuck her so hard that she can't walk for the next week. The way her ass looks with that pretty pussy peeking out has me sweating.

I get on my knees and take her ass in my hands, slap it, and lick her right ass cheek until she moans. I turn to the other cheek and do the same thing. Each time, the contact elicits a sexy moan from her.

Her pussy is calling to me, so I put both of my hands on her ass cheeks and spread them so I can see it. I slowly glide my tongue between her lips, and she arches her back, silently asking for more. I make love to her pussy with my tongue relishing every moan and twitch of her body. Becoming ravenous, I pull her ass forward more, needing to tongue-fuck her like there's no tomorrow.

"Say my name when you cum," I tell her, speaking directly into her pussy. Then I go back to licking and sucking and don't stop until she's shaking, moaning, and running to get away from my tongue. That's when I really bear down on that pussy until she's screaming my name.

When the aftershocks wear off, I smack her ass and say, "Don't move a muscle." I undress quickly and then slam into her, balls deep. There's no more time for taking it slow— it's been months!

I ram my dick into her repeatedly. I thrust more franticly as I feel her pussy tightening around me and we both cum at the same time. That shit was epic, and I swear I got a glimpse of heaven. When the waves of pleasure subside, we collapse onto the bed, panting.

I catch my breath and sit up to remove the tie and the belt around her wrists. Neither of us says anything as I pull her close and bury my face in her hair. I've missed everything about her.

Finally, I break the silence. "It's nice to meet you, Naomi."

"The pleasure was all mine," she says turning slightly to look at me.

I smile down at her and make the request that's been in my head since I saw her at that bar.

"Look, I know we need to talk about us, and I want to have that talk, but can we wait until after the wedding tomorrow?"

"I can do that," she says, and I feel instant relief.

Chapter Thirty-Eight

NAOMI

The look on Cassie's face when I walk into the rehearsal dinner on Vincent's arm is fucking priceless. The look I give her screams: "*Too bad, so sad. I won, bitch!*"

We go straight to where Pops and Patricia are sitting when Patricia notices us. She immediately jumps up screaming "you're here!" as she tackles me with a big bear hug.

She releases me after a few seconds, and steps back to take a good look at me. "Damn, girl! California did you good! You look amazing!"

"Stop it! I can't hold a candle to you — you're every bit the blushing bride."

"Who would've thought I'd ever be here? Vincent, let me steal Naomi away for a second. Girl talks and all that jazz."

"Not without giving the groom a hug first," Pops says, smiling and pulling me into a hug. "You're not the only one who's been waiting to see her." I get another hug, then he says "It's great to have you back. Now, before bridezilla steals you away there's another young man here who's been dying to see you," he says, pointing to Junior.

"Junior! I've missed you! Come here and give me a hug!" I say, with my arms wide open. He runs to me and gives me the hug I've been waiting months to receive. "Oh my God, I think you grew three inches! We have so much to catching up on. You want to sit by me during dinner so we can talk?"

"Yes!"

"Hey, what about me?" Vincent says, looking pouty.

"You'll survive," I say sarcastically. "I'll see you at the table after I talk to Patricia. Deal?"

"Deal."

Patricia motions me to the bathroom, and as soon as the door closes, I corner her. "I would've appreciated a heads-up about your evil stepdaughter who wants to get her claws into Vincent. What's up with her?"

"I know. I'm so sorry! I couldn't not invite her. I sent the invitation, but I never expected her to accept it. Last I heard, she was shacking up with some guy in Orlando. I guess she's got her sights set on Vincent now. I know she can be a b—"

"Bitch?" I supply, and she bursts into laughter.

"I was going to say a bit much. I'm sorry Naomi."

"It's okay, but I'm going to need something stronger if I have to put up with her and her snake eyes all day tomorrow." I say, and again Patricia bursts out laughing.

"Well, I'm just glad you're here. But seriously, you have transformed! You look Halley Berry hot! I know Vincent's jaw dropped when he saw you."

"You don't know the half of it." I say and proceed to tell her the story of how I came to be his date. When I finish, all she can do is stare at me.

"Shit! I should have stayed at the hotel, too! I'd have paid good money to see you shut her down like that."

"There's still time for that, don't worry."

"Well, regardless of anything, you and Vincent look happy together. I know he missed you every day. We are about to close on a house just around the corner from the boys, but it's been good, us being there with them. They were both heartbroken, and they needed us."

"I missed him and all of you too!"

"It's okay, I understand. However, now we have you back, and we're not letting you go again."

"I'm not going anywhere."

"Good."

"Now, what's our itinerary for this evening? I don't want to be accused of slacking on my maid of honor duties. Speaking of that, did you want a mini bachelorette party tonight after the rehearsal? We can go out."

"God, no. I'm too old for that."

"Please! You're forty-six."

"Exactly, I'm too old for that foolishness. I just want to be with my husband-to-be tonight. I've waited a long time for this, and I want to enjoy every moment."

"I understand."

"Now, let's get you back to your man." She says, as she pulls my hand.

***

The rehearsal went by without a hitch and before I knew it, it was over and so was dinner. I spent most of my time talking to Junior. When it was time to jump in with my maid of honor duties and make a toast, I fucking crushed it. It was so good that I could feel Cassie glaring at me the rest of the night. *Oh well, hater!*

After dinner, everyone breaks off into groups to talk and make their way to the open bar. I watch as Junior makes his rounds before leaving with the nanny.

I hate that he has to leave. I love that little boy no less, and I enjoyed every moment with him. I have every hope and intention of being in his life. Vincent and I give him one last hug before he goes, and we watch him go.

"You made his night, you know," Vincent says.

"No, he made mine."

"So, I didn't factor into it at all?" he asks with mock hurt feelings, and I laugh.

"Maybe a little."

"Well, allow me to correct that. Let's go."

"You want to leave *now*?"

"Yes."

"I'm the maid of honor, I can't leave early."

"Trust me, Patricia will not feel any way if I kidnap her maid of honor. She wants nothing more than for us to get back together so she can get her drinking buddy back."

After making him wait a few seconds, I smile and say, "Well, I'd hate to disappoint her. Let's say our goodbyes, then we can go."

"Oh, about that. I told Patricia we were leaving, and she said she'd see us in the morning — and we'd better not be late. Your makeup appointment is at nine o'clock sharp. C'mon, let's get out of here while no one is paying attention," he says, pulling me towards the exit as I laugh.

Chapter Thirty-Nine

NAOMI

The following day, I get up, showered, dressed, and kissed Vincent goodbye. I want to get to the makeup artist ahead of schedule. I feel like a slacker, so I'm trying to take my duties more seriously.

As I walk through the doors of their vacation home, there's so much activity I don't know where to look first. The mansion is stunning, and the wedding decor is extravagant. The funny thing is, I find I no longer feel intimidated by magnificent settings. *I've come a long way, and it's only going to get better,* I think as I see someone I don't recognize approaching me.

"Naomi, our MOH?"

"That's me."

"I'm Kelly, the wedding planner."

"Oh, it's nice to meet you. This all looks so magical!" I say gesturing to the decor.

"Thank you so much! Let's go, she's waiting for you."

Hours later, three stunning women — the bride, me, and the evil stepdaughter — are looking in the mirror, marveling at the magic that has been done. Having to deal with Cassie's foul attitude is a small price to pay to see Patricia's joy. I hope I experience something similar with Vincent one day.

There's a knock at the door, and the stylist yells, "Come in!" as she and her assistant makeup artist finish packing up.

"You three look amazing! Are we all done here?" Kelly asks the artists.

"They're snatched and wedding ready. Have a beautiful wedding day, Ms. Patricia!" the stylist says.

"Thank you so much! You did a great job," Patricia says, walking over to hug each of them.

"You're so welcome," they both say as they leave.

"Okay, perfect. We're right on schedule," Kelly says with a smile. Seriously, she's like J-Lo in *The Wedding Planner*.

"Is it time yet?" Patricia asks.

"After you get out of your robe, and get dressed, yes. Ms. Vergez, may I have a moment with you outside?"

"Why?" Cassie says snottily.

"If you step outside, I will expla—"

"Oh, just spit it out," Cassie says throwing her hands up in the air.

"Fine. Mr. Taylor informed me that you no longer have an escort as he will be escorting someone else. We have no time to find anyone to stand as your date for the walk down the aisle the pictures, or to sit at the table with you. So, I've moved you to the front row with the family." She says bluntly. I can't help but smile at how fierce she is.

"Excuse me? The front row? I'm her daughter!"

"Be that as it may, you won't be any less her daughter as a guest in the front row, which is where you are."

"Patricia! Are you going to let her do this to me?!" she screeches back at Patricia.

"I don't see why you'd mind considering the person you're really here for is no longer an option for you. You've never been one for family occasions, and you don't like me. In fact, I haven't heard from you in years, you don't respond to call or text. I'd say a wedding guest suits," Patricia says, shrugging her shoulders.

"Why don't you just lose gracefully," I say, surprising myself.

"Fuck you! You're nothing but a whoring housekeeper," she says with venom.

"Well, this housekeeper made the cut, and you didn't. Deal with it," I say as I turn away from her. Neither Patricia nor I even look back as she stomps off after the planner.

"Seems like being the maid of honor brings out the beast in me," I say, and once again we burst out laughing.

*****

The wedding flew by. The vows were beautiful, the photoshoot was fun, the dinner was delicious, but mostly I just loved being with everyone again.

When the festivities finally start to wind down, Junior's nanny once again comes for him, and Vincent and I walk them to the car. "Naomi, will I see you again?" He asks before they pull off.

"Of course! Friends for life!" I say and he smiles, sitting back in his chair in clear relief, and it does something to me. I have another family in these people, and I love them.

By the time we get back the newlyweds are out on the dance floor having their first dance. After the song is over others join them on the dance floor to *You and I*.

"They look so happy." I say to Vincent. When he doesn't say anything, I turn to see him staring at me. "Why are you looking at me like that?"

"Because you look happy, too. Would you like to dance, Ms. Miller?"

"Absolutely," I say, and take his hand so he can lead me to the dance floor. He twirls me and pulls me into his arms, and I feel like I have everything I've ever wanted when I look into his eyes.

The moment doesn't last long before someone asks, "Vincent, I need a moment with you." We stop dancing and I turn to see a frumpy man in a tux giving me a disapproving look.

"Wesley, it's a wedding. Can't you see I am occupied. What's so important that it can't wait until this dance is over?" Vincent demands.

"It's urgent."

"It damn well better be." Vincent says before turning back to me. "Business calls, but I'll be right back. Don't let anyone steal you away."

"Never." I tell him as he goes with the rude man. For some reason, I'm worried about why he's looking at me the way he is.

I decide to go to the bathroom to freshen up, but I get lost. I take the hallway to my left and search for a restroom. I turn a corner, and I see three doors two on my right, and one on my left. I figured one had to be the bathroom. As I walk by, I overhear voices, and almost immediately I know Vincent's is one of them, and he sounds pissed.

"He hinted at a hostile takeover if I don't end things permanently with Naomi. He said the board of directors would be very displeased if they had to clean up my image again because of her."

"I welcome him as a guest, and he makes threats at my wedding in my own fucking house!" *It's Pops he's talking to, not Wesley.*

"Do you think he's stirring the pot with the board?"

"It's possible."

"Can I be honest?"

"Always."

"I love the company, and I appreciate everything you've sacrificed for me, but I love Naomi more. I want a life with her. I don't want to have to choose between the love of my life and the company. I let her go once, and I can't do that again."

I hate what I just heard. Vincent is about to give up his legacy for me, and I don't want him to do that. *I need to get out of here think and process.* I turn back the way I came and run smack into someone.

"I'm so sorry," I say as I try to right myself and I look up to see Patricia, the beautiful bride.

"It's okay. Where are you going in such a hurry?"

"Patricia, I'm so sorry, but I need to go. I have to get out of here."

"Why? What's wrong Naomi?"

"I just have to go."

"Not before you tell me what's going on. Let's step into the office."

"No!" I say a little too forcefully. "It's already occupied."

"Okay, my room then. Let's go!" We make our way to her room, and I quickly tell her everything I overheard.

"Naomi, I understand why you feel the way you do, but I also want to point out that you'd be doing the same thing Vincent did. You know how it felt when your choice was taken away, so don't do it to him. He's a strong man, and he knows his own mind. Don't leave like this. I know you love him."

"I do, but what kind of love is it if I allow him to give up everything he's worked for? That's not love, it's selfishness. Tell Vincent something came up. I'm sorry to go like this, but congratulations! You're a beautiful bride. I'll stay in touch."

"Promise? Remember, I love you too, Naomi."

"I know, and I love you. Give Junior and Pops my love, too."

I go back to the hotel, change out of my dress and slip on some jeans, a t-shirt and a hoodie, then immediately start packing so I can leave.

Before I can finish packing, I hear a knock at my door. *I hope to God it's not Vincent, because I'll never be able to leave if he's here.* I look through the peephole and am immediately annoyed. I unlock the door and greet Cassie.

"What's wrong, Cinderella? It's not even midnight and you're already running?"

"I don't have time to deal with you. Say what you came to say and leave."

She folds her arms over her chest and smiles as she sidesteps me to peek into the room where it's evident, I'd been packing "So, you *are* leaving. Well, you're dumber than I thought. FYI: before you start spilling your secrets, make sure no one is around. You may hate me because I go after what I want, but at least I try. Look at you, packing and running away like a scared little girl. It's kind of disappointing — I thought you had more backbone than that."

"Are you done?"

"Yes. Apparently, you're a lost cause. Have a good life, Naomi Miller. Don't worry, I'll be there to help mend Vincent's broken heart. He'll be fine without you," she says as she turns and walks away.

I slam the door, mad at myself for letting her get to me. I take out a piece of hotel stationery and write a note for Vincent. I finish packing, check out, and go outside to the entrance where the valet parking and taxi concierge is, order a taxi, and run. Seems Olivia and Naomi aren't so different after all.

Chapter Forty

NAOMI

One Month Later

The time following my great escape has been awful, but productive. I decided to come back to my parent's house, because I still can't think of the house Vincent gave me as mine. I need to make a clean break from him. I made my decision, and I'd do it again because I love him that much. So, it's time to get my on with my life.

I'm in my room responding to the many emails from my book publishers, my gallery manager, and nonprofit organizations wanting to partner with me on the nonprofit foundation I am building using some of the money Vincent gave me.

Before I went to Mexico, I had finally decided that I wanted to tell my story, but in a book. I wasn't ready to talk to the media directly, but I could create a story mimicking my life. I decided to turn it into a love story. I had someone help me put together a synopsis, marketing plan, a cover, and I started reaching out to publishers. My name alone got me in the front door of five, and eventually I chose one.

I bought a space for the foundation in the downtown Holly-wood, Florida area and converted it into a gallery with the help of some of Pop's and Patricia's best people. It's set to open in a few months.

The foundation will be used to provide safe houses for survivors and/or victims of human trafficking, child laundering, and domestic abuse and guide them as they reclaim their lives and reach safety. I decided that it would be built in Connecticut, in the very spot where my story began, the former address of Redford Consultants LLC. It's only fitting.

I get up to use the restroom when I hear the house phone ringing, and I move to answer when I hear my dad pick it up. I was so preoccupied that I didn't realize he was already back from his trip. Mom is still on her three-day trip, and only on day one.

I hear my dad ask the caller angrily, "Who wants to know?" *Sounds like it's another reporter wanting to interview me.*

"Fine. I'll see if she's available," he grudgingly says. A few seconds later, I hear him wall up the stairs.

"Naomi?" he asks through the door.

"Yes?"

"Can I come in?"

"Sure."

"How are you holding up?"

"Great," I say sarcastically. "Isn't it obvious?"

"Yes, it is. Baby girl, why don't you just talk to him?"

"There's nothing to talk about. Being with me means he'll be forced out of his company, and I can't allow that. I love him too much to ask him to lose everything he's worked for just to be with me."

"Well, I think it should be his choice, he knows his own mind. I think you're underestimating him."

"Maybe. I guess I'll never know."

"You're so stubborn! You get that from me, by the way. All I'm saying is, think about it. Now, I've said my piece and I won't mention it again."

"Thanks, Dad."

"I actually came up here to tell you there's a producer from the *Diane Reaves Show* on the phone asking to speak with you. She wants to do a show with you, and she's offering to promote your book, foundation, and your gallery for free if you agree to appear as a guest and tell your story, live." he says, which gives me pause. "That would be good publicity, which would benefit victims all over the world, right?" He asks.

"Yes, it would."

"Well, do it for them. Look, you've spent enough time hiding out here. It's time to get back out in the world. Tell your story in your own words and stop all the speculating."

He's right. It's time to start moving forward with my life.

"Okay, I'll take the call."

***

Two weeks have passed before I know it, and I'm in New York at the studio where they do the *Diane Reaves Show.*

I'm waiting for my cue to come on stage, and I'm terrified. I look up at the monitor, and nearly panic as she starts to introduce me.

"Today, Naomi Miller will be joining us to tell us how she found out she's a victim of a child laundering ring. Don't go anywhere, because you don't want to miss this amazing story. Let's stand and give a warm welcome to Naomi Miller!"

219

The double doors slide open, and I'm suddenly frozen like a deer in the headlights. My eyes finally adjust to the studio lighting, and I try to relax and smile as I force my feet to walk over to the stage like I'd rehearsed earlier.

The crowd applauds encouragingly, and I finally get there and take my seat next to Diane.

"Welcome to the *Diane Reaves Show*, Naomi! Thank you for agreeing to tell us your story. I understand this is the first interview you've given since you learned about your past. I'm honored."

"Yes, it is. The media terrifies me," I say, and she and the audience laugh politely.

"Well, I certainly understand that. Some people can be complete vultures — but not me, I'm absolutely harmless."

"Right," I say jokingly, and the audience laughs.

"Oh, stop! It'll be painless, I promise."

"Okay, let's get on with it then."

"Let's start with Olivia Hunt. Where did the name come from?"

"My abductors. Their aliases were George and Cecilia Hunt. I found out later that their real names were Craig and Tasha Redford, and they were on the FBI's most wanted list. Their crimes included arson, kidnapping, child trafficking, human trafficking, extortion, and more. They ran their child-laundering and illegal adoption ring out of their business, Redford Consultant Services LLC in Connecticut back in the '90s. I was one of the many babies they abducted."

"I ended up becoming their "daughter" because the Redfords were tipped off the authorities were onto them and they fled, taking me with them."

"Wow. That's something. Do you know how they were able to steal you away from the hospital?"

"Yes, Tasha Redford disguised herself as a nurse claiming she needed to take me for a test the doctor ordered. My mom was tired, and she had no reason to suspect foul play, so she gave me to her. That was the last time my mom saw me until about a year ago."

"Wow, that's truly horrifying. Tell us what the Redfords were like as parents? What was your life like growing up with them?"

"They weren't good people, obviously. They never physically abused me, but the verbal abuse was bad. I've been working on healing from that and have recovered some repressed memories about Craig Redford while under hypnosis."

"What did you remember?"

"Attempted sexual abuse."

"Can you share more with us, Naomi?"

"Well, one memory was from when I was fourteen. I was in the bathroom getting ready to take a shower. I'd already taken off my pants and shirt when he came in, closed the door, and leaned up against it, just staring at me. Then he said, 'Take it off,' referring to my bra and underwear.

"When I didn't move, he started to walk towards me. He stopped in front of me and put his hand on my hip and slid it up slowly, then he groped my breast through my bra. I remember it hurt, and the smile he gave me when he saw he was causing me pain was so evil.

"Then, out of nowhere, Tasha slammed the door open. She was furious — not at him — at me. She yelled, 'Get out!' at her husband and he left the room right away. Then she turned back to me, and said, 'I always knew you were a whore. Don't you bat your slutty eyes at my husband ever again! Take your damn shower! Tonight, you'll repent for your sins.'"

"She made me stand in the corner all night and wouldn't let me eat anything the next day. She told me I'd better start wearing clothes that completely covered me if I knew what was good for me," I finish with tears rolling down my face.

"Oh my God! Can I get some tissues, please?" Diane asks someone off camera. Seconds later, tissues appear, and I take them and blot at my tears.

"I am so sorry that happened to you, and we admire your strength," she continues, with sympathy. "You're a survivor, and because of you, victims all over the world have an example to look up to." The audience applauds her statement enthusiastically.

Turning back to the camera she says, "Stay tuned! We'll be back with more of the Naomi Miller story."

A second later, the director yells "clear," indicating a commercial break. I'm immediately assaulted by a makeup artist who touches up my tear-stained makeup. Then, before I know it, we're back on the air.

"Let's continue, Naomi. Do you know where your abductors are now?"

"They're dead. They were killed in an accident back in 2015."

"Wow. Well, based on what we know about them, I'd say that was probably Karma making things right."

"Yes, I believe so."

"So, what happened next? Who took care of you after they were gone?"

"Well, after two days of watching the door, hoping it was a mistake, and it wasn't their car I saw being recovered from piles on asphalt where the bridge collapsed, I let the truth sink in that they were not coming back. I wondered how I'd go on without them, but decided I would survive, even though I didn't know how to do anything on my own.

"My saving grace turned out to be one of the few good things they did for me — they'd home-schooled me and did a decent job. I didn't have much in the way of social skills, but I knew enough to realize I could research anything I needed to know.

"The other advantage they gave me was they had remained practically invisible to the outside world. No one really noticed they were gone because I paid the rent on time, and they handled everything electronically, no one did. I just had to learn how to learn the ways of the word.

"It was easy enough to find a waitressing job in Miami that would pay me under the table. After that, I taught myself how to budget the money I made so I could manage the bills and I bought a cheap phone. When I needed to use a computer, I went to the public library down the block. I remained invisible, and I did what I had to do to survive."

"That sounds absolutely terrifying. I am in awe of you for having the strength to make it through that time in your life. Maybe you had a guardian angel."

"Maybe I did."

"Let's move on to a more pleasant subject. What was the reunion with your biological parents like, and how is your relationship with them now?"

"It was emotional and confusing, but undeniably amazing. They were instrumental in my journey to becoming Naomi. Every moment I have with them is a gift I cherish."

"That is beautiful. I'm sure they feel the same way."

"You know, initially, I didn't want to be Naomi Miller. I was up front with them about that when I first met them, and they didn't care. They just wanted to know me, whoever that might be. As the weeks went by and I got to truly know them, I changed my mind. Also, the thought of keeping the name my abductors gave me just didn't sit right with me. So, I decided to the name that was taken away from me, and embrace the emotional and spiritual journey that allowed me to adapt to my new reality"

"Is that all detailed in your book, *Finding Naomi?*"

"All that and more. In the book, a love story unfolds, as well as a motivational resource for survivors of trafficking and laundering. It gives readers and victims the steps to reclaim their lives. I was fortunate enough to have people around me who helped, but I realize not everyone has that. So, I want to them to know they can do it themselves, and that it does eventually get better. Most importantly, I want them to know they are worthy of love."

"Well, I'm sure your book will help women all over the world. I understand you've also set up a foundation for young women who were victims of trafficking?"

"Yes. Vincent Taylor gifted me the freedom to find my voice, and he was right to do so. When I started thinking about how many victims survive the same things I went through or worse with nothing and no resources or support system, I knew I needed to do something.

"My plan is to provide safe shelters all over the world, and partner with other organizations that can help these women, children, and men get their lives back. We'll help with paperwork, legal needs, housing, therapy, jobs, and whatever else is needed. Taylor Industrial will be building and designing all the shelters.

"I'm also opening an art gallery in a few months called Liv's Outlook Galleria, and the proceeds from all art sales will go to the foundation."

"Wow, you're a woman of many talents. Where will the art sold come from?"

"Right now, I'll be providing the art. I'm actually going to school to perfect my technique, and it's going well. I have amazing mentors."

"I'll just bet you do. Well, everything you're doing is simply amazing and it's going to change a lot of lives for the better. We wish you the best in all your future endeavors."

"Thank you, Diane."

"You're absolutely welcome. Now, let's talk about your relationship with the Taylors, especially one handsome CEO. Everyone wants to know the scoop on you and young Vincent Jared Taylor. Tell us, is the romance in your book based off you and your boss?" she asks, and I instantly freeze.

"I'd say he had a lot to do with it, yes."

"Tell us more, please!"

"Well, long story short, I met Vincent in August of 2019. I had an interview at Taylor Industrial and had practically been laughed out of there by the recruiters. I, of course, did not have the training, the technique, or any of the other qualifications for an internship there. I have always had a passion for drawing, but I had a particular undeveloped talent for drawing structures, but it was not enough.

"Afterwards, I tried to walk back home, but I got caught in the rain and couldn't. So, I ran into the nearest shop to avoid it, charge my phone, and wait it out. When inside, the proprietor of the shop approached me and allowed me to charge my phone in private considering my disheveled appearance. I sat down, and out of nowhere, Vincent appeared."

"He talked to me, asked me questions, and generally put me at ease which is good considering I was about to bolt. His demeanor was charming, relaxed, and I somehow knew I was safe with him. I told him about my day and the interview not knowing who he was at all, and he gave no indications it was his company that turned me away. By the time he was called away, less than thirty minutes after my arrival, he had offered me a job knowing I had lost out on one that day. Intrigued, I agreed to an interview the following day, and eventually, I started to work for him.

"What I did not know was he went back to his company and investigated what happened with my interview and why I had been turned away, and it was his specialist team that discovered that all my documents were fake. He knew this when he hired me and said nothing. However, he did have me investigated while I was working there, and for months, he found nothing.

"I worked for Vincent for seven months, and we had no issues until the pandemic hit. He gave me and only me the option to quarantine with him and his son and continue my employment. After that, our dynamic changed, we got to know one another, and we became more to one another.

"A few weeks into my moving in, Vincent's grandfather had a heart attack and we had to travel to LA to take care of him. While there, he admitted everything to me and told me who and what he suspected my parents to have been, kidnappers, launderers, and criminals. He had gotten that theory by simply talking to me, hearing me repeat things they said to me, and my fraudulent high-quality forgeries. Vincent wanted my permission to find the answers for me. I told him yes, and he did exactly that. As they say, the rest is history."

"Why do you think he did all that for you?"

"It's just the type of person he is. If he can help someone, he will. If he can fix a problem, he will."

"Wow, a sexy, successful billionaire with a good heart. That *is* rare. I'd say he more than fixed your problem. I wish I had a boss like that." she says, turning to the audience for their input. They all clap, laugh, and nod in agreement. "So, to clarify, he did not give you access to his bank accounts?"

"No, he did not, and if he had, I wouldn't have accepted it. I had everything I needed." I say confidently.

"Well, that is quite a story. We look forward to seeing great things from you, Naomi. We want to thank you for allowing us to be—"

"Actually, I'd like to add something else."

"Oh. Well, that sounds juicy, but we'll have to come back to that. We here at the Diane Reaves show, have a surprise for you; two very special guests who wanted to be here for you today. Everyone, please give a warm welcome to Naomi's parents, Andrea and Logan Miller!" she says as she claps and looks expectantly at the doors I came through earlier.

The doors open and reveal my parents. I watch as they walk towards us, hand in hand, smiling up at me. When they reach the stage, I stand and give them a hug. I didn't expect them to be here, but suddenly I realize I needed them here. Of course, there are a few other people I'd like here with me too, but nothing can be done about that now.

"Oh, you two are good!" I chide them, smiling. "We spoke on the phone right before I walked into the studio, and you didn't say a thing."

"We were backstage the entire time, watching." my mom says, smiling.

"We wanted to be here for you," my dad says.

"Thank you. You don't know how much it means to me."

"As you can see, it's all smiles and love on the stage tonight," the sneaky host says. "Stay tuned and we'll be right back so Naomi can say her piece!"

The camera zooms out on us, and the producer yells, "Clear!" The makeup crew is right there for touch-ups again. When they finish, I walk over to my parents and say, "You guys really had me fooled. Thank you so much for being here."

"We're proud of you and we'll always be here to support you no matter what you're doing," my dad says as he pulls me in for another hug.

"Okay everyone, clear the set please!" The director yells before walking over to us. "Mr. and Mrs. Miller, I have front row seats for you in the audience," she says, pointing to two vacant seats. I hug them once more and watch as they take their seats.

After that, I'm shooed back to my seat on stage to get ready for the last segment.

"Hello and welcome back to the *Diane Reaves Show!* We're talking with Naomi Miller. And I, for one, can't wait to hear what she wants to add regarding her relationship with young Vincent Taylor. Let's hear it!"

"I actually want to say something *to* him, not about him, if that's okay?"

"Just look at that camera there and tell him what you want to say," Diane says, indicating the camera aimed directly at me.

I take a calming deep breath. *Dad is right, I can do this.* "Vincent, before I met you, I didn't know what love was. Before you, I'd never had anyone show me what real love was. You were like a tsunami I had no idea how to defend myself against.

You excited, terrified, and challenged me with everything you made me feel. You blew me away with your kindness, and in the short amount of time I spent in your employ, and then the quarantine with you and your family — Pops, Patricia, and Junior — I experienced true happiness. Then, you went and found my family for me, and you gave it to me a second time. You are as much responsible for the woman I am today as I am.

"I was mad at you for a decision you made about me that I didn't understand until I was put in the same position. So, I want to apologize. On my journey to this moment, I've learned that people are imperfect — even you. What's become clear to me is this: the only thing that matters is us, that there is an us. You *were* right when you said my journey as Naomi was going to take a lot of therapy, time, and focus. However, I didn't need to make that journey alone. I don't want to make any more journeys without you by my side. So, in front of my parents and the entire world, I'm telling you that I love you, and if that life, love, and family is still waiting for me — I'm ready, Vincent."

Everyone, including the host is silent for a long beat when I finish. Diana finally takes her cue and says, "On that note, we're going to break for commercial, but we'll back with the Naomi Miller story. Stay tuned!"

Once again, I'm assaulted by makeup artists, and in the snap of a finger, we're live again.

"Naomi! You've given us the love story of a lifetime! What you said was simply beautiful, and it must've taken a lot of courage to say it on national TV."

"You have no idea," I say, smiling nervously. "I meant every word."

"I can see that. So, to clarify, you fell in love with your ex-boss?"

"I did, yes," I say, laughing at Diana's theatrics.

"Well, we have one more surprise for you. It's not my place to tell you, so I'll let him do it himself. Join me in welcoming Naomi's prince charming, Vincent Jared Taylor III — in the flesh!"

My eyes immediately snap to the closed double doors, and I simply forget to breathe.

Part 3

Chapter Forty-One

VINCENT

It's been a month since Naomi left the wedding, and me, with only a short note as explanation. It tore me up that she didn't say goodbye in person, but I couldn't find it in myself to really hold it against her — I know she meant well just like I did. But, she was right about one thing, even with that knowledge, it still hurts.

I hate her choice, especially since Pops and I got things under control and there was no real reason for her to leave. We got enough of the board on our side to ensure no threat of a hostile takeover was possible, ever. Oh, and I got the honor of doing the fun part – firing Wesley.

Things have settled down, the company is back on track, and now it's time to win my woman back. This time, I have to ensure she knows that no work, no company, no person will ever come between us.

Pops and Trish just got back from their honeymoon two days ago and flew directly from Saint-Tropez to meet Junior and I in New York, and I am so thankful they did.

We're all backstage in our own room watching Naomi on the monitor while waiting for them to call me up.

Just looking at her makes my fingers twitch with a need to touch her, and today, she looks even more beautiful. I'm scared shitless.

"Are you nervous?" Pops asks, coming up behind me.

"Are you kidding? I'm about to lose my shit!"

"Good."

"Good? Why is that good?"

"It means that she's the one for you. I had that feeling both times I went down the aisle, and it never led me wrong. She's going to say yes. Just speak from your heart."

"Thanks, Pops," I say as I pull him in for a hug.

"She's an extraordinary woman, and she loves you. I'm so happy for you two," Patricia says as she joins in with the hug.

"Well, that is quite a story. We look forward to seeing great things from you, Naomi. We want to thank you for allowing us to be—"

"Actually, I'd like to add something else."

"Oh. Well, that sounds promising and juicy, but we'll have to come back to that. We here at the Diane Reaves show, have a surprise for you; two very special guests who wanted to be here for you today. Everyone, please give a warm welcome to Naomi's parents, Andrea and Logan Miller!" she says as she claps and looks expectantly at the doors I came through earlier.

I hear a knock at the door, and someone says, "Mr. Taylor, we're ready for you." Shit, that's my cue, but I'm more interested in what she wanted to add before Diane cut her off and brought the Millers out. I had no idea her parents would be here, but I'm happy they are, nonetheless. It will make this moment even more special.

I move to the area behind the sliding doors and look up at the television mounted, and continue to watch the show, and I get the shock of my life.

"Vincent, before I met you, I didn't know what love was. Before you, I'd never had anyone show me what real love was. You were like a tsunami I had no idea how to defend myself against, and you excited, terrified, and challenged me with everything you made me feel. You blew me away with your kindness, and in the short amount of time I spent in your employ, and then during the quarantine with you, your family — Pops, Patricia, and Junior and especially you — I experienced true happiness. Then, you went and found my family for me, and you gave it to me a second time. You are as much responsible for the woman I am today as I am.

"I was mad at you for a decision you made about me that I didn't understand until I was put in the same position. So, I want to apologize. On my journey to this moment, I've learned that people are imperfect — even you. What's become clear to me is this: the only thing that matters is us, that there is an us. You were right when you said my journey as Naomi was going to take a lot of therapy, time, and focus. However, I didn't need to make that journey alone. I don't want to make any more journeys without you by my side. So, in front of my parents and the entire world, I'm telling you that I love you, and if that life, love, and family is still waiting for me — I'm ready, Vincent."

I stare at the screen, stunned, barely paying attention to anything being said when the doors open. All I know is the look on Naomi's face is everything I was hoping for and more. Everyone else fades into the background and I just want to throw her over my shoulder and take her home with me.

When I step onto the stage, the audience quiets down, and Naomi looks up at me in disbelief. "How are you here right now?"

"Well, as it turns out, I have some things to say to you too. So, I reached out to the show, and they invited me. I had a little inside help." I say, eyeing Logan in the crowd.

As she realizes who I'm pointing to, I can see her putting the pieces together. She turns back to me, and I nearly lose every thought in my head. *It's time, now or never.*

"Naomi, I have loved you from the moment I laid eyes on you. I know I've screwed some things up, but my heart was and always will be in the right place when it comes to you, I promise.

"My feelings for you will never change. I want all of you, Naomi Miller. There's no future for me that doesn't include you. So, will you do me the incredible honor of becoming my wife?" I ask as I get down on one knee and pull out the ring that I had custom-made for her. I've never been so happy and so afraid of rejection in my life.

"Yes! Yes! Yes! A thousand times, yes!" she screams.

After I slide the ring on her finger, I stand, take her in my arms and kiss her like my life depends on it.

"Okay, there you have it! The perfect happy ending to the Naomi Miller and the billionaire story! Be sure to head to social media to give us your thoughts on tonight's show. I'm Diane Reaves, and I'll be seeing you."

"We're clear!" The director yells, and the stage erupts into chaos around us.

I feel a tap on my shoulder, and turn to see Patricia, Pops, and Naomi's parents standing there. I didn't realize this moment could have been more perfect, but it just happened. There's one face missing though. "Where's Junior? Did you bring him?"

"Of course, we did, he's right behind me," Pops says turning to reveal him, but he's not there.

"I'm sure he got swallowed up in all the commotion. I'll go find him," I say, and for some reason, I feel unsettled.

Chapter Forty-Two

VINCENT

Fifteen minutes later, we've all gone over the entire set, the bathrooms, and every nook and cranny where he could be hiding, but I can't find him. At this point, I'm in full panic-mode as is Naomi.

The audience has been cleared from the set and only the production crew are left finishing up for the day. The police arrive and are now running the security footage from all the entrances and exits to the studio trying to see if he left the building.

Just as I'm about to lose what's left of my patience, one of the cops comes over and says, "Mr. Taylor, we found something. Come take a look at this."

Naomi, Pops, Patricia, and the Millers all trail behind me as I follow him.

"I want you to look here," the officer says, pointing to a monitor. He pushes play and we can see the crowd of people clapping and surrounding us on stage. A few seconds later, we see Pops, Patricia, and Junior walking toward the stage. Junior is behind Pops when suddenly, someone dressed all in black reaches out, grabs him, puts his hand over his mouth, and walks out of the camera's view with Junior, and no one even noticed.

"He knew exactly where the cameras were. We have to assume this was an inside job, and a professional." The officer says.

"Could you rewind it and zoom in, please? I think I saw something," I say. "Freeze it there. Look, he's dressed in the exact same shirt as the camera staff. Is that a badge on the shirt? Can you read the name?"

"Let me zoom in," the operator says. After a few seconds, we have a clear visual of the badge, and it reads "Nolan Wright."

"I know Nolan, and that's not him. He's a sweet guy. He'd never be a part of something like this," Diane says from behind us.

"Okay. I need a background check on this guy, as well as an address. If he's not a part of this, then something might have happened to him," the lead detective says to a uniformed officer. "Do you have any enemies, Mr. Taylor?"

"Lately, yes," I say, thinking of all the people I've pissed off recently.

"I'll need a list so we can question them and get alibis. Miss Reeves, how many people knew the Taylors would be guests on today's show?"

"The entire staff," she says, just as a uniformed officer walks in.

"Lieutenant, we found this stuck on the windshield of Mr. Taylor's rental car," he says as he hands a piece of paper to the detective. He takes a second to read it, before handing it to me.

> You think you can get rid of me that easy? Well, the fucking joke is on you. You will give me what I want, or your precious son will have an intimate knowledge of exactly what your slut went

> through. Call the cops and he's lost to you forever. Don't test me.
> I want my $2 million by tomorrow — in cash. I'll contact you
> with instructions.

"I know who has my son," I say, my voice dripping with disdain.

"Okay, Mr. Taylor. I'll need a picture of your son, and everything you know about the kidnapper. We need to put out an Amber Alert ASAP."

"My lawyer will give you everything he has. I'll call him now."

"Sir, who do you suspect?"

"Lauren Cavendish, his birth mother."

***

A few hours later, we're all back at my Airbnb. Thank God I chose this over a hotel because the space is needed. I sit and watch as the detectives set up shop, prepping for when Lauren makes contact. They've put a tap on my phone lines as well as Pop's.

I've never felt so damn helpless in my fucking life! How the fuck does a mother even do this to her own son for money? She's clearly unhinged!

If she does anything to Junior, there is no place on this earth where she can hide. I will destroy her, and her whole fucking family, too!

I can't sit still, so I go up to the room Junior slept in, wanting to feel near him. I sit on the edge of his bed as I give Lawrence a call.

"Mr. Taylor, I've just touched down in New York. I'm picking up my rental now, and then I'm headed to the Crown Plaza. Is there anything you need?" He asks.

Instantly, I feel a little relief knowing he's close by to get me out of jail if shit hits the fan.

"No, not now, thank you. I wouldn't have asked, but I appreciate you coming here more than you know."

"You didn't have to, it's my job. The moment I got the call from the police, I booked my flight. I know how much you love your son, and I'll help you get him back any way I can. You and the police have direct access to me."

"Okay. I do need help with something, actually. Tell me what you've got so far on Lauren."

"I've made some calls to see if anyone knows where she or her family are living. Apparently, Lauren parted ways from her family years ago. A source of mine claims that she may have acted as an informant to the feds against her own family as well as a handful of other crime syndicates and organizations. Her parents are more than likely hiding out seeing as their home is in foreclosure, and all their accounts have been frozen. If my sources are correct, she's in survival mode, and is trying to get out of dodge. I don't know exactly what they were into, yet, but whatever it is, it's big. That's why she showed up on your doorstep needing money."

"I don't care how desperate she is, you don't do what she's done. When we find her, I want every book thrown at her — kidnapping, extortion, blackmail, and anything else you can come up with!"

"Consider it done, sir."

"Thank you. One more thing, and it's an unconventional request. I need information. So, if you have any resources who work on the … opposite side of the law — use them to find out who would be interested in Junior. Find out what kind of people and organizations we may be up against. I don't care what it cost or what laws are broken to achieve our goal. Junior is all that matters. Can I trust you with this?"

"Yes sir. I know someone."

"Good. Reach out to them as soon as possible. I need to prepare for the worst and hope for the best. Things are never really as they seem when it comes to that lunatic."

"I'll contact you as soon as I know something, sir."

"Thanks, Lawrence. Oh, and Lawrence?"

"Yes, sir?"

"I just asked you to break the law for me, so I think our dynamic has changed. Call me Vincent."

"Understood. I'll be in contact, Vincent." he says with enthusiasm. It's possibly the first time he's ever shown any emotion when we've talked.

Truthfully, I don't know what I'd do without Lawrence Terrell. He's young for a corporate lawyer — two years younger than me — but he's as sharp as they come. He's been an asset since the day I hired him. That was probably one of the best decisions I ever made for the company and myself. At this point, he's probably the closest thing I have to a friend too, since he knows all my secrets.

I lay back on Junior's bed and start to think about the facts. *Lauren is beyond desperate, and she's just made her position worse by fucking with us.*

These thoughts fill me with despair, so I just lay there, staring up at the ceiling. I'm so lost in thought that I don't even notice the door opening.

"I figured I'd find you here." He says as he comes in and sits down on the bed with me.

"Any new developments?" I ask, without looking at him.

"They found Nolan Wright in the trunk of his car. He'd been knocked on the head and now has a pretty bad concussion, but he'll live. He's given the detectives a description of the man who assaulted him."

"God! This is a fucking nightmare! What if we can't find—" I say my voice breaking.

"Don't think like that. Junior needs you to be strong and have faith. You're scared, and I am too. We've got to keep it together for his sake. We *are* going to find him, I promise you," he says, pulling me into his arms. For the first time since I was a kid, I cry while he holds me in his arms.

Chapter Forty-Three

LAUREN

"Where is he?"

"In the trunk," Joe says as he steps out of the car.

"Why the fuck is he in the truck? Get him out of there!"

"Cut the bullshit. You're a heartless bitch and you don't have a maternal bone in your body. You don't give a shit about that kid, you're only out for yourself. Besides, if you expected me to ride around with a billionaire's kidnapped kid in my backseat for all to see, you must really think I'm stupid."

"I don't give a fuck what you think. Get him out of there now!"

"Happily. *After* I get my money."

"Here's half of what I promised — twenty-five thousand dollars."

"Bitch, I didn't agree to half. I want it all. Right now! You have two minutes to give it to me."

"Relax, you'll get the money when they pay me. Trust me, they'll pay whatever I want for him, I guarantee it. Now, open the trunk."

"I knew I couldn't trust a bitch who makes her money on her fucking back. You gave me your word, and you're breaking it. So, like anyone else, you'll pay the price for lying to me. The only difference is, I'm not going to kill you, not this time. I want my fucking money." he says menacingly.

Shit! Shit! Shit! Should've just given him the fucking money! From the look in his eyes, there's no fixing this, but I have to try anyway. I already have a target on my head, no reason to add more. "Look, I have the rest, just let me get it."

"I'll take that as a deposit," he says, grabbing the bag with the three grand in it, "and the kid too."

"*Deposit?* What the fuck do you mean a deposit?"

"I mean you went back on your word, so the rules have changed. You call me when they pay the ransom, and I'll bring the kid back to you, unharmed. Oh, and I don't want fifty anymore, I want seventy-five. If I don't get it by tomorrow, you don't get him."

"Seventy-five thousand dollars, Joe! How the fuck do you jump from ten grand to fifty?!"

"Since you tried to fucking cheat me! You tried to double-cross the wrong guy, so now the price has changed. Call me when you've got my money." he says as he opens his car door.

"You have twenty-four hours. Don't make me wait too long, I might get restless. I have a few friends who would love to get their hands on this little boy of yours if only to have leverage over a powerful family like the Taylors. Tick tock, Laurie." He says before getting in his car and speeding away. As he does, I feel like my freedom is speeding away with him.

Fuck! I'm in over my head. I need a backup plan. If anything happens to Junior, I will never be safe from Vincent. Vincent has to pay the ransom. Joe's not bluffing, I could see it in his eyes. *Shit! Think Lauren, think!* And then it hits me. I know exactly what to do.

Chapter Forty-Four

NAOMI

Today has been a roller-coaster of emotions, ending with a huge drop into a pit of despair. What should've been one of the best days of my life, is now one of the worst. How could Lauren kidnap her own son and hold him for ransom? How evil is this woman?!

Just the thought of how terrified Junior must be makes me sick to my stomach.

The detectives working to find Junior have set up an entire command post at Vincent's Airbnb. They're prepared for when Lauren makes contact, but it's been hours and we've heard nothing. Everyone is sick with worry. Patricia's had an anxiety attack and has gone to collect herself. Vincent is here, but no one has seen him for a while, and Pops just went looking for him.

I feel so alone right now. I walk to my former bedroom, close the bedroom door, curl up on the bed, and cry. I'm sobbing so hard I almost don't hear my phone ringing. I pull it from my back pocket and see a number I don't recognize. Something tells me to answer it anyway.

"Are you alone?" the caller asks, and I immediately recognize it as Lauren's voice.

"Where's Junior?"

"Are you alone?"

"Tell me where he is bitch."

"Look, we don't have time for this. The longer you question me, the more danger he's in."

"What do you mean?! He's with you, isn't he?!"

"No, plans changed. I fucked up. You have to get away and bring me the money without alerting anyone else or Junior will end up dead or worse."

Whatever it takes, I will get Junior back. "When and where?"

After she sends me the location, I quickly change, grab a large bag, and make my way downstairs. I need transportation and my car is not here, so I take the keys to Vincent's rental. More than likely, the rental agency has a tracker on the car. When Vincent figures out that I've left with his car, he will start looking for me, remember the tracker, and follow me with the police. I'm counting on Vincent to figure it out in time because Junior's life, and possibly mine, depend on it. It's a leap, but I believe in him. I grab the keys and head out to the garage. The place is so chaotic that no one notices me leave.

My first stop is one of my bank locations to make a withdrawal. I'm not rich, but thanks to the financial advisor Vincent referred, I've invested some of the money Vincent gave me, and it's multiplied nicely.

After waiting for what seemed like hours, the bank finally releases the money to me, and I walk out of the bank with two million dollars.

After leaving the bank, I follow Lauren's instructions to the letter and drive to Apotheke Chinatown in New York City. I park close by on the street, pay, and walk into the bar.

Upon entering, I look around for Lauren and when I don't see her, I head directly to the bar and take a seat. I place the black bag in between my seat and pull my chair up so that no one notices it. I order a shot of vodka for courage as I wait for the she-devil.

"So, you *can* be a good little maid and follow instructions," Lauren says snidely as she comes up behind me.

I turn on my stool and see she's wearing sunglasses, a hoodie, jeans, and some Adidas. I can barely control the disgust I feel for her and can't help baiting her a little. "Well, well, well, look who's slumming it. Did you run out of Gucci, or did you have to sell it all along with your soul?"

"Touché, Molly-Maid," she says.

"Where's Junior?"

"I'll get him to you after I get the money."

"Or I can signal the cops to move in on this establishment and hand you over to them," I say, bluffing my ass off.

"Do that, and you run the risk of never seeing him again. He will be sold to the highest bidders for leverage over the Taylors. Do you know how organized crime works? Everyone would try to get their hands on him. Is that what you want? This is no game! If I don't get the money to the guy holding him, he'll sell Junior!"

What scares me most is not what she's saying, but the desperation in her voice. She's scared, and I think for once, it's not for herself.

"Who has him? Give me a name."

"I can't. He'll kill me."

"The minute you're able, you'd better take that money and run fast and as far away as you can. If Vincent catches up with you, I'm not sure what will happen. Giving me the guy's name will distract him and give you a head start. You'd just better pray that guy hasn't done anything to Junior. If he has, Vincent will be gunning for you and a head start won't matter. So, once again, who is he?"

"His name is Joe Middleton. He worked security for my family."

"Call him and tell him you have the money."

Chapter Forty-Five

VINCENT

Pops eventually convinces me to come out of the room, and the first thing I do is look for Naomi, but she's nowhere to be found.

"Pops, did you see Naomi?"

"No, I haven't. Has anyone seen Naomi?" Pops asks the policemen and detectives in the room.

"I think I saw her leave."

"Leave? Did anyone ask where?"

"No, we figured she wanted to drive and clear her head."

"Something's up. She wouldn't just leave like that without saying anything. Did you put a tap on her phone?" I ask the lead detective.

"No, sir."

"Shit! Call the rental agency and see if the tracker on the car is live and have them track her. I think Lauren has made contact, with Naomi. Someone, pull up her phone records in the last two hours to see if anything stands out. If she didn't tell me she was contacted, she has a reason. We have to get to her." I tell them and they all fly into action.

I'm coming baby, hold on.

I immediately call Lawrence back. "I just sent my location, how far are you from me right now?"

"About twenty minutes."

"Shit! Naomi left, I have no idea when, and I have reason to believe Lauren contacted her. She's in my rental, and it has a tracker in it. I'm trying to find her. I need you on standby in case you're closer to her than I am. Can you do that?"

"Absolutely. When you get the location, send it to me."

"It's coming.

I either need someone to tail her or a hacker to track her — I'm sure that's why she took my car— she *wants* me to track her, meaning she needs reinforcements and may be in danger. We have to figure this out, now.

Chapter Forty-Six

VINCENT

They tracked the car in New York City, near a bar called Apotheke Chinatown. I'm thirty minutes away, about to leave now, how far are you? I just sent you the location." I ask.

"Let me check." He says, and I wait and pray he's close by. "I'm twelve minutes away. I'm headed there now."

"Okay, I'm on the way too. The cops will follow behind us. Please don't lose them."

"I'm on it." He says before disconnecting the call.

***

"Vincent, I have eyes on the car. I don't see her or Lauren. I'm going to go into the bar close by and see if I see them there."

"Shit! I still have another nineteen before we get there, but the police have been dispatched. Hopefully, they make it before I do."

"Okay, stay on the phone, I'm going to connect you to my Bluetooth."

Chapter Forty-Seven

LAWRENCE

I walk into the bar, and I immediately locate the two women talking. Lauren, the piece of work, seems to be making a snide remark, but Vincent's woman is standing her ground and making some of her own if I'm correctly reading the facial expressions and body language.

I walk over to an empty table in the middle of the restaurant and sit.

"Can I get you a drink, sir?"

"Yes, I just need a moment." I say to the pretty waitress who approaches me two seconds after I sit down.

"No problem. I'll come check on you in a few." She says as she sashays out of sight.

"Vincent, can you hear me?" I say into my Bluetooth as I pick up the menu. I am starving actually.

"Yes. Do you see them."

"I do. I've posted at a table where I have a direct line of sight. They are having a conversation and it doesn't seem to be going well."

"Do you think Junior's there?"

"No, I doubt any exchange besides the verbal ones they are throwing at each other will take place here. They're waiting for something or someone, I just don't know what."

She had a black backpack when she came in, but now I don't see it. The money must be in the bag. Wait, if she didn't get the money from you, where did she get it?" Lawrence reports.

"My guess is from her bank. She's made some good investments, she got an advance from her publishers, and she has at least two more sources of passive income that I am aware of. It's her money she's using to get Junior back."

I respect the hell out of this woman. She's been through a lot, and she just keeps persevering. She's here, risking her life; she's giving her money to save a child that is not hers. Vincent is a lucky man.

Besides, this is easily becoming the most excitement I've had since becoming a corporate lawyer for Taylor Industrial. Working for Vincent Taylor III is certainly nothing like I expected, and neither is the man himself. Vincent isn't like most trust- fund kids I've known throughout college. He doesn't hide behind his title, and if something needs to be said or done, he does it. Vincent won't ask anyone in his company to do something that he won't do, and that inspires loyalty in his people, in me.

Granted, we just got to first name basis, but regardless of that, he and his grandfather have been my pseudo family since I started here. I haven't had anyone like that in my life for a long time.

Honestly, when he asked me to outsource to someone on the other side of the law, I almost laughed. I definitely know the perfect guy for the job — me. It's time to put some of my Harvard-honed hacker skills to use. I haven't done that for a while but hacking into Lauren's info was a piece of cake. The skills came right back, like muscle memory.

For the last two years, Lauren's been staying in hotels and living off the mysterious deposits hitting her account each week since mid-2019. When I tracked the money, I found out it was sent by different companies, all owned by rich, powerful, and sometimes political men and women. Still, the money can't be too good if she's stooped to blackmail, extortion, and the kidnapping of her own son.

I don't think Lauren has the brains or the guts to pull this off by herself. I think there's a puppet master involved behind the scenes, but who? The guy who kidnapped Junior? That's the only thing that makes sense. This whole thing strikes me as a plan that has gone sideways and now the greedy cunt is scared. When I see Lauren take out her phone and make a call, I get ready to move.

Chapter Forty-Eight

NAOMI

"I have your money. Where do you want to meet?" Lauren asks the person she's called.

"The parking garage a few streets over from the bar," I hear the faint reply as I eavesdrop.

"Wait, you're here? You followed me?"

"You didn't really think I'd trust you again, did you? Fool me once and all that shit. Come and meet me, Laurie, and bring her with you too."

Lauren ends the call and stands up, looking around franticly. "He's been watching us. He wants to meet, and he wants me to bring you with me. Come on, we have to go now," she says with more than a little panic in her voice. She even grabs my arm to hurry me along. She's definitely scared, and that tells me I should be too.

Shit! I need to buy some time for Vincent and the cops to get here. I think as I pray for a miracle.

I stop walking abruptly, and Lauren turns around and glares at me. "Why does he call you Laurie?" I ask, glaring right back at her. "Is he an old boyfriend or something?"

"Do us both a favor — don't ask questions you can't handle the answer to. Now, let's go."

"Not until you answer me."

She crosses her arms and stares at me, obviously pissed that she couldn't scare me into dropping the subject. I cross my arms, mimicking her, and wait. A few seconds go by before she gives in, realizing I'm not budging until she tells me what I want to know.

"Fine. My parents hired Joe after what happened with an… associate of theirs."

"Hire him to what?"

"To … keep the clients from damaging the product- me, and all the other Cavendish girls they traffic. I, being their daughter, was only offered to a select few of course."

Oh my God!

"And these clients are—?"

"Not important. Besides, they will get theirs one day, I will make sure of it." She says and, in this moment, I can see the vulnerability and pain in her eyes. I suddenly second guess everything I ever thought about her and realize there's more to her story.

"I don't want your pity!" she screams at me when she notices the look on my face. "That's not why I told you. I'm not like you. I'm not a fucking *victim!* I did what I had to do to survive!"

"And you think that I didn't?"

"I don't have time for this bullshit! Do you want the kid or not?"

"The kid is your son!"

"He was never *my* son — he was a prison sentence. Now, he's going to earn me my freedom."

"I know you think that, but that's not what's going to happen. He can't free you from your parents' bad decisions or all the things that have gone wrong in your life. Money can't fix everything. He's a child, not a pawn. God does *not* smile down on selfish, evil people. Eventually, you'll reap what you've sown. Or maybe I'm wrong and there's still a chance you might be a decent person," I say as I start walking again.

"Save your sermons for Vincent. I don't need your fucking advice," she says as we walk into the parking garage. There's a stairway leading to the second level right in front of us, so we take it, instead of waiting for the elevator.

At the top of the stairs, we keep going, heading toward the other side of the garage. When we're almost there, a car honks and flashes its lights at us, scaring the shit out of me. I recognize the man behind the wheel of the car. It's the man from the security footage.

He gets out of the car and walks up to us. "Where's the money?"

"In the backpack," Lauren says, handing it to him.

"Open it."

"Where is Junior?" I ask.

"Don't worry, I keep my word, unlike your partner here. She's the reason you're in this mess in the first place. Fucking cunt isn't worth the trouble," he says, looking at Lauren like he's daring her to object. When she says nothing, he smirks and walks over to his SUV, opens the hatch and lifts Junior out.

I run over to him, reaching out for Junior, but the thug pulls him away. The jerking motion is enough to rouse Junior, and when he opens his eyes, he looks lost until he sees me and calls my name. Then, he starts struggling to get out of the man's hold.

This guy is dangerous, I can see it in his eyes. I realize I have to keep Junior calm, so I say, "Hey, I'm here! You're going to be okay; I promise." To my relief, he stops struggling just in time, because I can see his captor is losing patience.

"I'm going to put you down. When I do, I want you to walk over to that woman there," he says, pointing at Lauren.

Junior looks at her and then at me. "I want to go with Naomi."

"Lauren, come and get your brat, and get out of here."

"I can take him," I say desperately.

"You could — *if* you were leaving. You've presented an even better opportunity and I plan to take advantage of it. You're worth way more than the kid. It's being said that your fiancé would do anything for you. Well, let's put that to the test," he says, causing my stomach to roll.

"Joe, that wasn't the deal." Lauren says, finally speaking up.

"Shut the fuck up. Just take the kid and leave, or you won't make it out of this garage alive," he says as I step away and position myself.

"Lauren, go. Keep your word and get him to Vincent, no matter what," I say.

"No," she says, surprising me and pulling my attention to her.

"Fucking bitch!" I hear him say as he reaches for something in his back pocket. I don't wait to see what it is, I just react. This was the chance I was waiting for

"Junior, *run!*" I yell a second before striking the goon's throat with as much power as I can. I don't want to kill him, just incapacitate him. My hit is perfect, and he goes down slowly, clutching his throat and dropping his gun.

When he's down, I take his head in my hands and thrust my knee up into his face, knocking him out cold. I kick the gun out of the way. Turns out all those sessions my trainer insisted on were useful after all.

When I'm sure he won't be getting back up, I look around for Junior. He's standing with Lauren, a few feet away from her car. I pick up the gun, still keeping my eyes on the downed man, and walk backwards to Lauren and Junior.

When I reach them, I grab Junior and hug him hard, looking at Lauren over his head. "You'd better go now," I say, giving her an out since she finally acted like a human being.

I shift my focus to Junior, and don't even look at her as she gets into her car. Before she can get it started, I hear police sirens approaching. Lauren puts the car in gear, floors it, and almost makes it to the exit. Before she can escape though, she's stopped by two police cars that pull in and block her.

"Hands up," the cop says over the loudspeaker. "Get out of the car slowly, then get on your knees with your fingers locked behind your head."

I thought Lauren would put up a fight, but she does as she's instructed, and in seconds the cops are out of their vehicles and one of them is cuffing and mirandizing her.

The other cop comes over to check on Joe. "He has a pulse," he yells to his partner. "We need paramedics."

Suddenly, I see Vincent running towards us.

"Dad!" Junior screams, running to him and jumping into his arms. Vincent catches him, scoops him up, and continues hurrying toward me. I'm a little afraid of how angry he's going to be with me, until I see the look on his face.

When he reaches me, he stuns me by pulling me into a tight embrace with the arm that's not holding Junior.

"You're not mad at me?"

"I can't be. What you did was out of love for my son. There's really only one thing I want to say to you," he says as he sets Junior down.

"What's that?"

"Thank you for bringing *our* son home safely. I love you both so much," he says, hugging us again.

"I love you, too! I'll always do what's necessary to keep you and him safe. Always." I tell him, still running high on adrenaline.

"I'm going to hold you to that."

"I'm counting on it." I say, with a smile on my face and love in my heart.

Chapter Forty-Nine

LAWRENCE

I can't help but be impressed by Naomi. She's the real deal.

I didn't have to lift a finger. She took that guy out in seconds with a fucking throat punch!

When I see things are under control, I hang back. No need to let the cops know I was here the whole time. I wait until they've got Lauren in cuffs, then it's safe for me to make an appearance.

I walk up, and when Vincent sees me, he says, "Lawrence, thank you so much! I appreciate everything you did."

"Of course. Just doing my job."

"No, this was much more. At this point, you're more like part of the family than an employee," he says, smiling like I haven't seen him do in a long time.

"So, this is the infamous Lawrence?" Naomi asks as she approaches us.

"The one and only," I say.

"Wow, I was expecting you to be… old," she says, and I can't help but laugh.

"Yeah, that seems to be what most people expect when they meet me."

"Wait, why are you here?" she asks, looking back and forth between Vincent and me.

"Lawrence has been tracking you the entire time until I arrived with help," Vincent says.

"It turns out, I wasn't needed. She took down that thug like a pro."

"You're joking!"

"No, she really did, Dad. I saw it, and it was awesome!" Junior exclaims as he runs up to us, and everyone laughs.

"So, I've got a Ronda Rousey on my hands?" Vincent asks, and Naomi laughs.

"Yeah, and you better watch yourself!"

"I love you, Naomi."

"I know you do. I love you too," she says and kisses him.

Seeing their love in person gives me hope that maybe there's someone out there for me. I'm not sure where that thought came from. When I think about it though, the concept sounds pretty good.

"Why don't you go ahead and hit the road," I say. "I'll clear everything up with the police and give them my statement. They can contact you later if they need anything else."

"Wait," Naomi says. "This is the gun I took from Joe over there. You may want to give it to the police."

"I'll get it to them. Thanks."

"Got any plans for dinner after you're done here?" Vincent asks.

"Um, no. Why?"

"Well, you do now. We'll see you at six o'clock sharp."

"I'll be there." I say as I walk away smiling. I guess happy endings happen after all, maybe even for me. Guess we will see what the future holds.

Epilogue

NAOMI

February 1, 2021

Finally, life everywhere has gone back to normal as there's a vaccine for the virus. My life is anything but normal — and I love it! I've been promoted to *wife* of the billionaire, I'm founder and president of the Olivia Hunt Organization, owner of two art galleries, and a *New York Times* bestselling author. My life has truly become the fairytale I never believed was possible for me!

I'm moving on to the next chapter in my life — being a mother of twins. Vincent doesn't know that yet. I'm ten weeks pregnant and I'm putting together a reveal he will never forget. His new assistant, whom I adore, is in on it, and she has ensured the entire floor where Vincent's office is located is empty so I can slip in and prepare things while he's at lunch. He's due back any time.

I quickly get out my speaker and queue up on the song we made love to on our wedding night. I shed my trench coat and lay it on the chair near to the door. I looked for two weeks straight before I found the perfect costume for today. He'll know what it means immediately.

The sexy stockings I found look amazing with my Christian Louboutin. Today, we are role-playing the best story of all, *The Billionaire is a Daddy!*

Thank you for reading!
I hope you enjoyed the story.

Please leave a short review on Amazon, or my website,
DIAMONDSNWATSON.COM.

Quarantine
with the Lawyer

Please enjoy this sneak peek…

"I'm sorry, I didn't mean it like that, Lauren."

"Don't insult me, Lawrence. You meant exactly what you said. I can see your disgust clearly, but I can also see the lust in your eyes. I can imagine how inconvenient it is that your dick gets hard for me, your best friend and employer's ex and son's mother, a whore, and a kidnapper. What Vincent would think about you wanting to fuck me?"

"Listen, even if my dick does get hard for your body, the thought of your heart, your manipulation, and your recklessness makes it go soft just as quickly. Now, I extended this offer on behalf of Vincent, and that is the only thing I will be doing with or for you. So, no need to worry about me being "inconvenienced.""

"You're a good liar, Lawrence, but then you have to be because you're a lawyer. Here's the thing — you're not good enough in this case. I know the look you're giving me all too well," she says as she reaches under the table and runs her fingers up and down the straining erection I refuse to acknowledge. "I know you're not one for breaking rules, but maybe just this once you can toss the rulebook out the window."

I remain still and say nothing, as I inwardly struggle not to drag her out the chair and onto my lap. My silence is obviously the reaction she's looking for. She takes me by surprise when she slides under the table, unbuckles my pants, and in seconds sucks my dick into her warm, wet mouth. Damned if I don't almost cum immediately.

When I look down and see her eyes looking up at me as she licks my tip like a lollipop, I already know that I've lost the round, but not the war…

Game on, Maneater.

Quarantine with the Lawyer

Book Two of the Quarantine Trilogy

DIAMONDS NICOLE WATSON

Diamonds is a new author in the Women's Fiction genre. She is a lover of all things romantic, and steamy.

Find out more by going on my website:

DIAMONDSNWATSON.COM

D.N. Watson